MOTHER OF CARMEL

MOTHER OF CARMEL

A Portrait of
St. Teresa of Jesus

E. ALLISON PEERS

SCM PRESS LTD

For my God-daughter

ELIZABETH

'¿Quién or trajo acá, doncella,
Del valle de la ristura?'
'Dios y mi buena ventura.'

334 01035 7

First published 1945
by SCM Press Ltd
58 Bloomsbury Street, London wc1
Reprinted three times
Reissued 1979
Printed in Great Britain by
Fletcher & Son Ltd, Norwich

CONTENTS

Foreword   7
Principal Abbreviations   8

PART ONE

PREPARATION

I At the Incarnation: Teresa of Ávila (1515–1557)   9
Birth—Childhood—Boarding school—Profession—Illness—Spiritual conflict—'Second conversion'—Contact with the Society of Jesus.

II At St. Joseph's: Teresa of Jesus (1557–1562)   27
Conflicts with confessors—Visions and voices—Meeting with St. Peter of Alcántara—First thoughts of a Discalced Reform—Opposition to the project—Its abandonment and resumption—Foundation of St. Joseph's, Ávila.

PART TWO

ACHIEVEMENT

III The Life: A 'Book of the Mercies of God' (1562–1565)   46
The *Life* fundamental to a knowledge of St. Teresa—A spiritual autobiography—The little treatise on the Four Waters—The *Relations*, a pendant to the *Life*.

IV The Way of Perfection (1565 ff.)   61
Circumstances of its composition—The two autographs—A tripartite plan: domestic exhortations; the life of prayer; commentary on the Paternoster—The most vigorous of her books, written at the height of her powers.

V From Medina to Pastrana (1567–1569)   79
Visits to Ávila of Maldonado and the General of the Order—Approval of further foundations—The Medina foundation (1567)—St. Teresa enlists Antonio de Heredia and St. John of the Cross—Malagón and Valladolid (1568)—Toledo and Pastrana (1569).

VI   From Salamanca to Seville: the Exclamations
     and Conceptions (1570–1575)   95
     The *Exclamations of the Soul to God*—Foundations
     at Salamanca (1570) and Alba de Tormes (1571)—
     St. Teresa on her journeys—St. Teresa Prioress at the
     Incarnation (1571–4)—St. Teresa and St. John of
     the Cross—The *Conceptions of the Love of God*
     (*c.* 1571–5)—Foundations of Segovia (1574), Beas and
     Seville (1575).

VII Persecution. The Foundations. The Interior
     Castle (1576–1577)   120
     Conflict between the Observance and the Reform—St.
     Teresa goes to Toledo and begins the *Foundations*
     (1576)—The *Interior Castle* (1577): a survey of the
     Mystic Way.

VIII The Last Journeys (1577–1582)   142
     The storm at the Incarnation (1577)—The conflict
     within the Order continues, and ends with its
     partition—Fresh journeyings and fresh foundations:
     Villanueva de la Jara and Palencia (1580); Soria
     (1581); Burgos (1582)—Death at Alba de Tormes.

PART THREE

FAME

IX   Teresa the Writer   165
     She appeals both to the ordinary person and to the
     scholar—The *Letters*—The *Poems*—Her prose not
     always easy, but always terse, virile and vigorous—
     Purity of her language—Figures of speech—Variety
     of style.

X   Teresa the Saint   179
     She writes of her own experiences—Earnestness and
     sincerity of her language—Her personality: charm,
     simplicity, virility—Her sanctity: often unrecognized
     because of her complete naturalness—Teresa the
     Mother of Carmel, and of many souls outside it.

     Index   190

FOREWORD

Two years ago, in *Spirit of Flame*, I told the story of the little Carmelite friar, St. John of the Cross, and discussed the appropriateness of his teaching to the world of today. This companion volume attempts a portrait of his great collaborator, St. Teresa of Jesus.

Once more I have tried to stand back, and, whenever possible, to use the words of Teresa herself. As she wrote a great deal about her life, the chief difficulty has been that of selection: so attractive are her books, and the accounts of her bequeathed to us by her contemporaries, that it would have been far easier to write a large biography of her than a small one. In particular, it has been very hard to avoid crowding the canvas with names, so numerous, and so sharply and fully delineated in the Spanish narratives, are the people with whom she came into contact. By omitting all mention of many of these, I have attempted to concentrate the reader's gaze upon the few who were closest to her, and, most of all, upon herself.[1] I hope that the result will be to arouse that kind of interest in her which sends readers to her own writings, in which they will find a still clearer reflection of her vital personality.[2]

E. A. P.

University of Liverpool,
January, 1945

---

[1] See *A Handbook to the Life and Times of St. Teresa and St. John of the Cross* by E. Allison Peers (Burns, Oates and Washbourne, 1954) for a history of the Discalced Carmelite Reform, biographies of the principal persons connected with St. Teresa, and other studies (Ed., 1961).

[2] See *St. Teresa of Jesus and Other Essays and Addresses* (Faber and Faber, 1953) for some further studies by Professor Peers (Ed., 1961).

PRINCIPAL ABBREVIATIONS

FOOTNOTE abbreviations of St. Teresa's own works are: F., *Foundations*; I.C., *Interior Castle*; L., *Life*; LL., *Letters*; R., *Relations*; W.P., *Way of Perfection*. Arabic numerals after LL. refer to the number of the letter in the Spanish edition of P. Silverio de Santa Teresa (Burgos, 1922–4). Roman numerals after any of the other abbreviations refer to chapters. Where bracketed numerals are added, they refer to the volume and page in my edition of the *Complete Works of St. Teresa*, abbreviated C.W. Thus L. IX (I, 54) means 'Life, Chapter IX (*Complete Works*, Vol. I, p. 54).' By *Studies* is meant my *Studies of the Spanish Mystics* (London, 1927–30, 2 vols.).

All the translations from St. Teresa are my own: those from the *Letters* have been specially made for this book; the remainder are from C.W., occasionally with slight verbal modifications demanded by the context.

PART ONE

PREPARATION

I

AT THE INCARNATION: TERESA OF ÁVILA (1515–1557)

ÁVILA.

To those who have known it, the name calls up associations which are unique. Yonder it stands, on the bare Castilian plateau, higher above the sea than the summit of Snowdon. Glimpsed from afar, its grim mediæval walls, with their round towers, seem in the clear air to have sprung erect out of the barren soil. Within those walls, there is little grace: everything speaks of strength, fortitude and determination. And well it may, for was not 'Ávila of the Knights' for centuries a front-line post in the struggle of Christians against Moors? Its very Cathedral, built into those massive walls, looks less a house of prayer than a fortress. And the austere, soaring lines of that fortress seem to dominate the architecture of the entire city.

How fitting that Ávila should have given birth to that woman-saint—'for masculine courage of performance,' as Richard Crashaw puts it, 'more than a woman'—whose charge to her daughters in religion was 'Be strong men,' and who, writing verses for them to sing at their festivals, more than once chose martial themes and measures through which one seems to hear the tread of that mighty army, the Church of God:

> *All ye who with our Master fight,*
> *And 'neath His banner take your stand,*
> *Oh, sleep not, sleep not, 'tis not night:*
> *There is no peace in all the land.*[1]

Not that there was anything martial or austere about Teresa de Cepeda y Ahumada's childhood. Quite the contrary. The large family into which she was born on March 28, 1515, was one accustomed to comfort. There were numerous servants—and Teresa's father could have afforded to buy slaves, had he ever been able to bring himself to keep them ('On one occasion,' relates Teresa, 'when he had the slave of a brother of his in the house, he was as good to her as to his own children').[2] There were books about the place—the Bible, Virgil, Cicero, pious literature and contemporary poetry—and that, in the sixteenth century, denoted easy circumstances as well as culture. There were well-to-do relatives in the city and district. All the indications were that little Teresa would enjoy a sheltered childhood, make an early and successful marriage and settle down to produce a family as large as her own, in an atmosphere, perhaps of affluence, and certainly of leisure.

And these indications are emphatically not belied by anything which she tells us of her own character. True, when she 'played with other little girls,' they 'used to love building convents and pretending to be nuns,'[3] and to Rodrigo, the brother so near her in age who, among her eleven brothers and sisters,[4] was her chief playmate, she would confide a predilection for the life of a hermit and build hermitages with stones in the orchard. But, in a country and an age where a woman's normal career was

---

[1] *Poems*, XXIX (III, 309).
[2] L. I (I, 10).
[3] L. I (I, 11–12).
[4] Her father, twice married, had two sons and a daughter by his first wife, and seven sons and two daughters by Teresa's mother, his second.

marriage or the life of religion, playing at convents would be as usual as playing with dolls, and it was as natural that a devoutly brought up little girl should build hermitages as that a manly little boy should parade his tin soldiers. And, anyway, relates Teresa, with charming naïveté, the stones they heaped up 'at once fell down again; so we found no way of accomplishing our desires.'[5]

There is, of course, the well-known story referred to by Teresa, amplified by her chief biographer, Ribera, and for English readers immortalized in a poem by Crashaw, of how Teresa and Rodrigo discussed the possibility of becoming martyrs and 'agreed to go off to the country of the Moors, begging our bread for the love of God, so that they might behead us there.'[6] Today that aspiration sounds most heroic, even when qualified by Teresa's dry admission: 'but our greatest hindrance seemed to be that we had a father and mother.'[7]

> *Farewell, then, all the world! Adieu.*
> *Teresa is no more for you.*
> *Farewell all pleasures, sports and joys*
> *(Never till now esteemed toys).*
> *Farewell whatever dear may be,*
> *Mother's arms or Father's knee.*
> *Farewell house and farewell home!*
> *She's for the Moors and martyrdom.*[8]

Yet it should not perhaps be taken too seriously. In another land and age, children gifted with initiative and imagination would have run away to look for pirates or become brigands, and Nurse, administering salutary

[5] L. I (I, 11).
[6] *Ibid.* According to Francisco de Ribera *(Vida de Santa Teresa de Jesús,* I, iv), they were found by an uncle, not far from their home, and taken back to their parents.
[7] *Ibid.*
[8] Richard Crashaw: 'A hymn to the name and honour of the admirable Saint Teresa.'

smacks, would opine that 'it's all along o' them books you're for ever reading.' Well, it was all along o' them books which Teresa—an apt scholar—was for ever reading:

> We used to read the lives of saints together; and, when I read of the martyrdoms suffered by saintly women for God's sake, I used to think they had purchased the fruition of God very cheaply; and I had a keen desire to die as they had done, not out of any love for God of which I was conscious, but in order to attain as quickly as possible to the fruition of great blessings which, as I read, were laid up in Heaven.[9]

That was the motive—reward. A perfectly understandable one. Teresa was only a child. Let us not attempt to make her more than she was—an absolutely normal child, growing up, at an earlier age than northern children do, into a young woman with quite a natural and healthy degree of worldliness.

She said her prayers, of course, and even 'tried to be alone' when she said them. She gave her tiny alms. In her childish way she would talk with Rodrigo of the eternal verities and she liked to indulge her sense of mystery by repeating, 'again and again,' a phrase which had captured her imagination: 'For ever—ever—ever!'[10] When her lovely mother died, worn out by child-bearing, at thirty-three, she sought consolation by appealing to the motherhood of Our Lady. But other emotions supervened. She was thirteen then; just beginning, as she says, to become aware of her natural graces,[11] and she went through a phase, common to most normal girls, of personal vanity:

> I began to deck myself out and to try to attract others by my appearance, taking great trouble with my hands and hair, using perfumes and all the vanities of this kind I could get—and there were a good many of them.[12]

[9] L. I (I, 11).
[10] *Ibid.*
[11] L. I (I, 12).
[12] L. II (I, 13).

She began to discard lives of saints and to bury herself in voluminous and fantastic novels of chivalry: 'I was never happy unless I had a new book'[13]—how refreshingly human! She became intimate with some cousins of about her own age whose frivolous chatter did her no good and with an older relative whom her mother had attempted in vain to keep out of her house and who appears to have done her more harm than anyone else, though she also found the servants 'quite ready to encourage her in all kinds of wrong-doing.'[14] In short, she confesses, 'I lost nearly all my soul's natural inclination to virtue.'[15]

It was trivial enough, no doubt, save when viewed in retrospect from the summit of Mount Carmel, but we shall better understand Teresa the woman if we remember that she had been a charming and attractive girl and had suffered from all the defects of her qualities. When her mother was dead and her only elder sister—a half-sister, Doña María—had married, her father grew concerned about her, and sent her as a boarder, at the age of about sixteen, to a local finishing school, attached to the Augustinian convent at Ávila, St. Mary of Grace. Home-bred, she began, 'for the first week,' by disliking boarding school intensely; but she goes on to confess (again so ingenuously!) that this was 'not so much from being in a convent as from the suspicion that everyone knew about my vanity.'[16] But, the initial shock over, she found herself happier than before. She had an irresistible way with her ('The Lord had given me grace, wherever I was, to please people') and so she 'became a great favourite.'[17] The routine was agreeable; the nuns were kindly and pleasant; and there was one in particular who succeeded

13 Ibid.
14 L. II (I, 15).
15 Ibid.
16 L. II (I, 16).
17 Ibid.

in gaining the girls' genuine affection. Yet, though (as might have been expected) this nun frequently extolled the religious life, Teresa not only developed no sense of vocation, but actually felt 'the greatest possible aversion from being a nun'[18] herself. True, she confesses to a natural trepidation at the idea of the conventional alternative,[19] but it seems probable that she was at that time more or less resigned to it.

During the eighteen months which she spent at the school her strong antipathy to the religious life weakened to a vaguer distaste. 'I could not persuade myself'[20] to enter it, she says of her feelings at this period. It was an extraordinarily obstinate will that Our Lord had set out to conquer. The next step came after she had been sent home for a time with a 'serious illness.'[21] As soon as she got better, she went to pay a visit to her married half-sister, in the country, and, on the way there, stayed for some days with an uncle, who made her read 'good books in Spanish' to him, and evidently influenced her a great deal. 'I did not much care for his books,'[22] she admitted, and they were presumably of an ascetic type, for what they chiefly inspired her with was the fear of hell. It was by this 'servile fear,' she says, 'more than by love,' that she was eventually led to the cloister.

> I began to fear that, if I had died of my illness, I should have gone to hell; and though, even then, I could not incline my will to being a nun, I saw that this was the best and safest state, and so, little by little, I determined to force myself to embrace it.[23]

Not very heroic—not exactly in the spirit of that famous Spanish poem:

[18] *Ibid.*
[19] 'I was also afraid of marriage': L. III (I, 17).
[20] L. III (I, 18).
[21] *Ibid.*
[22] L. III (I, 18).
[23] L. III (I, 18–19).

I am not mov'd, my God, to love of Thee
By Heav'n which Thou dost pledge me as reward.
I am not mov'd to cease to grieve Thee, Lord,
By thoughts and fears of Hell which threaten me.[24]

As a child, Teresa had been moved by hopes of Heaven; as an adolescent, she was swayed by thoughts and fears of Hell. Yet, in her mature life, she was to be surpassed by none for her complete selflessness.

As to the exact date on which Teresa entered the Carmelite Convent of the Incarnation at Ávila, there has been a considerable difference of opinion. This is not the place for a detailed discussion of the matter and I will merely say that my own view is based mainly upon a statement made by the Saint in 1576: 'It is forty years since this nun took the habit.'[25] Literal acceptance of those words, which are supported by other allusions of this kind, as well as by external evidence,[26] would give us the year 1536; and, as the day of her entry was All Souls' Day (November 2), it would have fallen just over seven months after her twenty-first birthday. She was professed exactly a year later.

The last stages of the five-year conflict with herself had been excessively painful. 'When I left my father's house,' she avers, 'my distress was so great that I do not think it will be greater when I die. It seemed to me as if every bone in my body were being wrenched asunder; for ... I had no love of God to subdue my love for my father and kinsfolk.'[27] But, once the decision was made, the change that came over her was so sudden as to appear miraculous. Sweeping floors might seem a poor exchange for bedecking herself to go to parties—and to her reason it did still. But her emotions were thrilled by the perfect

[24] It has been attributed to St. Teresa, but it is certainly not hers. For the full text, see *Studies*, I, vi.
[25] R. IV (I, 319).
[26] Cf. C.W. I, 20, n. 2.
[27] L. IV (I, 20).

freedom which issues from complete surrender: 'there came to me a new joy, which amazed me, for I could not understand whence it came.'[28]

Yet this joy did not mean perfection; on the contrary, 'for almost twenty years'[29]—she specifies this period on several occasions—she was only half converted. Not till she was about forty-two years of age did the beginnings of sanctity appear in her. To use a favourite image of her own, she was a plant of slow growth, and needed a great deal of watering.

About these 'twenty years on that stormy sea'[30] of interior conflict not a great deal need, or indeed can, be said. The first thing that happened to her was a breakdown in health. Even before entering the Incarnation, she had suffered from 'serious fainting fits, together with fever.'[31] The new mode of life increased their frequency, and she also developed 'heart trouble,' as well as 'many other ailments.'[32] As the convent had no strict rule of seclusion, her father was able to arrange for her removal, when she had been there for nearly two years, to a village named Becedas, 'where they had a great reputation for curing other kinds of illness and said they could also cure mine.'[33] Their 'drastic remedies,' however, caused her 'the greatest tortures.' Debilitated, unable to eat and racked night and day by 'intolerable pain,' she returned home, only to be given up by the doctors as 'consumptive.'[34]

This was in about July, 1539, the 'cure' having extended from April to June.[35] On the night of August 15

---

[28] L. IV (I, 21).
[29] *Ibid.*
[30] L. VIII (I, 48).
[31] L. III (I, 19).
[32] L. IV (I, 21).
[33] L. IV (I, 22).
[34] L. IV (I, 22), L. V (I, 30).
[35] From this point onwards I follow my own chronology without attempting to justify it in any detail.

came new trouble—a prolonged fit which seems to have been cataleptic. Confronted with so alarming a phenomenon, sixteenth-century medical skill was powerless. The young nun was pronounced dead—indeed, in one of those graphic touches which so enliven her autobiography, she tells us that when she eventually recovered consciousness she found wax on her eyelids.[36] A grave was dug for her in the convent grounds, and, for a day and a half, the sisters awaited her dead body.[37] By the mercy of God, however, she escaped being buried alive, and at the end of four days came to herself again. Here is her own vivid description of her 'intolerable sufferings':

> My tongue was bitten to pieces; nothing had passed my lips; and because of this and of my great weakness my throat was choking me so that I could not even take water. All my bones seemed to be out of joint and there was a terrible confusion in my head.... I could move, I think, only one finger of my right hand.... They used to move me in a sheet, one taking one end and another the other.[38]

In this state she remained from August until the following Easter. As nothing could be done for her, she returned to the convent—an apparently confirmed invalid at twenty-five. For nearly three years more her paralysis, though gradually improving, crippled her: 'when I began to get about on my hands and knees, I praised God.'[39] Not until her fortieth year did the effects of it entirely leave her.

But, to counterbalance these physical trials, Teresa had been enjoying spiritual experiences which were the foundation of many more to come. She had been withdrawn from the convent in the autumn of 1538, and for some unspecified reason (possibly to allow her to gain strength) the cure was not to begin until the following spring. For the intervening months she went on a visit to

[36] L. V (I, 31).
[37] Ibid. Cf. Ribera, op. cit., I, vii.
[38] L. VI (I, 32).
[39] Ibid.

Doña María, the married half-sister with whom she had stayed previously and whose house was not far from Becedas. On the way, she called on the uncle to whom she had read 'good books in Spanish,' and this time he gave her one for herself—'a book called *Third Alphabet*.'[40]

Teresa had no longer to confess to a lack of interest in devotional literature; and it is not surprising that she should have been attracted by the *Third Spiritual Alphabet* of the Franciscan, Osuna,[41] for it can be read with pleasure to this day. Dealing with the lower rather than the higher stages of the contemplative life, and thus appealing particularly to beginners, its main concern is with the exercise of recollection, and in particular with that stage of the contemplative life known as the Prayer of Quiet. Though over-discursive and unmethodically arranged, it abounds in attractive and telling imagery and often carries the reader away by the sheer force of its eloquence. One can well imagine its effect on a girl who knew little of method in prayer, and nothing of recollection: 'I was delighted with the book,' she wrote, 'and determined to follow that way of prayer with all my might.'[42] The copy which she used, it may be added, is still preserved in her Avilan convent. Its 'yellow pages bear the traces of constant study. Whole passages are heavily scored and underlined, whilst on the margins a cross, a heart, a hand pointing (her favourite marks), indicate the quaint thoughts and tender conceits which seemed to her the most worthy of notice.'[43]

Of so skilled a teacher Teresa proved to be an apt pupil. Previously the contemplative life had been a sealed

---

[40] L. IV (I, 23).
[41] It has been translated by a Benedictine of Stanbrook (London, 1931) and is described in some detail in *Studies*, I, 78–131.
[42] L. IV (I, 23).
[43] Gabriela Cunninghame Graham: *Santa Teresa*, London, 1907, p. 100.

book to her. Following Osuna's leading, however, she passed through the stage of meditation and in time was raised to the Prayer of Quiet—'and occasionally,' she adds in her *Life*, 'even to Union';[44] but there, it seems clear from other parts of her works, she was mistaken. As a rule, during the whole of these twenty years, she confined her spiritual exercises to meditation: except after Communion, she 'never dared begin to pray without a book';[45] and whenever she discarded the book she experienced distractions and aridity. Nor, during those years, did she once find a confessor who understood her, though she was continually looking for one. It is hardly to be wondered at, in such circumstances, if her interior progress was slow.

In more fundamental respects, too, her spiritual life was far from satisfactory. Since sanctity, the deeper it grows, becomes ever the more conscious of its failings, it is understandable if, looking back after a quarter of a century of progress, what it sees fills it with horror. But even allowing for this it is clear from Teresa's account of these years how much of what we should normally credit her with she still lacked. Had she lived in an enclosed convent she might have progressed more rapidly.[46] But at the Incarnation the sisters had a great deal of freedom. They could go out of the convent, which stands about half a mile beyond the city walls; they could receive visitors and accept presents. They were treated with deference, referred to as 'ladies' and addressed as 'Madam.' They were allowed to organize little festivals in honour of their favourite saints. So it was quite natural that, as Teresa grew better in health, she should turn once more to semi-worldly habits—harmless enough, perhaps, for those who live in the world, but unbecoming in any who have taken the vows of religion. She 'began to

[44] L. IV (I, 23).
[45] L. IV (I, 24).
[46] So she herself thought also (L. VII: I, 38).

indulge in one pastime after another, in one vanity after another and in one occasion of sin after another.'[47] And not only did she progress no farther in the contemplative life, but she was 'ashamed to return to God and to approach Him in the intimate friendship which comes from prayer.'[48] She would, of course, recite the petitions assigned to her by her Rule, but prayer in the sense of communion with God—mental prayer, which 'in my view, is nothing but friendly intercourse, and frequent solitary converse, with Him Who we know loves us'[49]— she gave up for a time altogether.

It was during these dark days—to be exact, on Christmas Eve, 1543—that Teresa suffered the grief of losing her father. Into the early chapters of her autobiography Alonso Sánchez de Cepeda enters quite frequently, though only for brief moments. It is evident that he was a man of strong personality, who quite overshadowed his second wife, Teresa's pretty and submissive mother, and of whom Teresa herself, as a child, stood in proper awe. Neither she, for example, nor presumably her mother, had any intention of being caught reading novels about the heroes of chivalry. Yet he was no martinet, but a kind father, a considerate master and 'a man of great charity towards the poor.' Unswervingly truthful, he was never heard either to 'swear or speak evil.' And he was 'a man of the most rigid chastity.'[50]

During the last years of his life the stern Don Alonso and his daughter drew much nearer to one another and she gives us a beautiful picture of their growing intimacy. Beneath his irreproachably devout and moral life, she felt, there was something lacking, which, fortified by the experiences to which the reading of Osuna had led her, she yearned to communicate to him. So 'by indirect

[47] L. VII (I, 37).
[48] Ibid.
[49] L. VIII (I, 50).
[50] L. I (I, 10).

method'[51]—how well one can imagine the tactfulness of her approach!—she set about his instruction. First, she gave him books and left him to read them. Then, to her delight, he began to grow responsive. Eventually he capitulated, and within a very short time[52] was firmly treading the road of contemplation. 'He often came to see me, for he derived great comfort from speaking of the things of God.'[53] Their mutual trust and confidence had grown complete.

All this took place before Teresa abandoned her practice of mental prayer; and, after she had gone for a year or more without returning to it, she felt bound in honesty to tell him so, giving her illness as an excuse, which, crediting her with his own rigid standards of truthfulness, he accepted without question. It must often have caused her tender conscience great remorse to have deceived him, for his last illness, during which she was able to tend him, was a very brief one. The simple words in which she describes her state of mind will strike a chord of sympathy in many a reader:

> Distressed as I was, I forced myself into activity.... I was so determined not to let him see my grief... that I behaved as if I felt no grief at all. Yet so dearly did I love him that, when I saw his life was ending, I felt as if my very soul were being torn from me.[54]

And now there comes a period in Teresa's life—from 1543 to 1555—about which we know next to nothing, probably because there is next to nothing for us to know. What little she tells us herself is concerned wholly with her spiritual condition during the time she had ceased to

---

[51] L. VII (I, 42).
[52] 'Five or six years (I think it must have been),' says Teresa, characteristically (L. VII: I, 42), but it cannot have been quite so long, for it was only towards the end of 1538 that she saw Osuna's book for the first time, and barely five years after that Don Alonso was dead.
[53] L. VII (I, 42).
[54] L. VII (I, 44).

lean 'upon this strong pillar of prayer.'[55] Her description of this period as a 'stormy sea'[56] is not merely
conventional. Instead of making spiritual progress, she
was like some tiny ship tossing on the waves, alternately
falling and rising again, only to fall once more. Her
allegiance was divided between God and the world, for
which reason she found neither joy in the one nor
pleasure in the other. 'When I was in the midst of
worldly pleasures, I was distressed by the remembrance
of what I owed to God; when I was with God, I grew
restless because of worldly affections.'[57]

In such an atmosphere mental prayer could not be
expected to flourish. 'Very often,' she confesses, 'over a
period of several years, I was more occupied in wishing
my hour of prayer were over, and in listening whenever
the clock struck, than in thinking of things that were
good. Again and again I would rather have done any
severe penance that might have been given me than
practise recollection as a preliminary to prayer. . . . Whenever I entered the oratory . . . I had to summon up all my
courage to make myself pray.'[58]

Some of St. Teresa's biographers have glossed over
these confessions as though they had no meaning. I
believe, on the contrary, that, like her descriptions of her
childhood, they should be given full weight if we are to
appreciate the immense power of the appeal which she
was to make, in later years, to the immature and the
spiritually imperfect. A stained-glass saint might have
written the *Conceptions*, the *Exclamations* and even some
parts (though not many) of the *Interior Castle*—but not
the *Life*, the *Foundations* or the *Way of Perfection*.

The quickening of St. Teresa's spiritual life, often
described as her 'second conversion,' began, about the

[55] L. VIII (I, 48).
[56] *Ibid*. Cf. p. 16, above.
[57] L. VIII (I, 48).
[58] L. VIII (I, 51).

year 1555, in two ways. One was the return of a sense of God's presence, more vivid than anything she had previously known. 'I could not possibly doubt that He was within me or that I was wholly engulfed in Him,'[59] she wrote ten years later; but we cannot at this stage entirely trust her self-diagnoses, for she seems sometimes not to have distinguished between her actual experiences and things that she had been taught or had read. 'I believe,' she continues, in the context just quoted, 'it is called mystical theology';[60] and goes on to describe the operation of the soul's faculties in language which is obviously taken from her reading. But of the reality of her experience we may be certain and its nature seems fairly evident. She had passed from the Prayer of Quiet to the threshold of the state which she was later to describe as the Fifth Mansions, the Spiritual Betrothal or (less happily, since the term implies a permanence which she had not then attained) the 'Prayer of Union.'

A second new experience consisted of visions. As early as 1539,[61] Teresa had had a revelation of Christ, 'in an attitude of great sternness,' showing her what there was in her that displeased Him; a vision, she tells us, which she saw, not with her bodily eyes, but with the 'eyes of the soul'—'and it made such an impression upon me that, although it is now more than twenty-six years ago, I seem to have Him present with me still.'[62] But about 1555 visions and voices began to become part of her normal experience: she started, as she put it, 'to see certain visions and experience revelations'[63]—still, and throughout her life, with 'the eyes of the soul': she never had corporeal visions—and also to 'think she was some-

[59] L. X (I, 58).
[60] L. X (I, 58).
[61] The reference (quoted in the text) to 'twenty-six years ago' (L. VII: I, 40) decides the date.
[62] L. VII (I, 40).
[63] R. IV (I, 320). The date is fixed by the reference in this passage—it was twenty-one years before the *Relation* was written (1576).

times being addressed by interior voices.'[64] Perhaps this
phenomenon was due partly to the habit which she was
developing of 'trying to make pictures of Christ inwardly'[65]—a practice which I cannot help thinking may
have been inspired by the methods of 'visible meditation' used by the Society of Jesus. Further, she developed
her visual powers by gazing at natural objects—'a field,
or water, or flowers'[66]—and finding that they 'reminded
her of the Creator': 'I mean,' she explains, 'they
awakened me, helped me to recollect myself and thus
served me as a book.'[67] Her inability to meditate
intellectually, to which she frequently refers, had no
doubt helped to retard her spiritual growth, and
evidently, to some extent, this newly discovered faculty
took its place. At first she could only picture to herself
things that she had actually seen: 'If I did not actually
see a thing, I could not use my imagination, as other
people do, who can make pictures to themselves and so
become recollected. It was for this reason that I was so
fond of pictures.'[68]

It was during this period that Teresa was given a copy of
St. Augustine's *Confessions*, and it can be imagined how one
who had developed that habit of visual meditation would
be affected by the narrative of St. Augustine's conversion.

> When I started to read the *Confessions,* I seemed to see myself in
> them.... When I ... read how he heard that voice in the garden
> it seemed exactly as if the Lord were speaking in that way
> to me.[69]

Soon afterwards, as we shall see, the Lord did begin
to speak to her. But, before this happened, she was to
receive help from another quarter.

Not long previously the Jesuits had founded a house

64 *Ibid.*
65 L. IX (I, 54).
66 L. IX (I, 55).
67 *Ibid.*
68 L. IX (I, 56).
69 L. IX (I, 56).

in Ávila—a fact which makes it still more likely that St. Teresa owed her habit of visual meditation to the *Spiritual Exercises*. It is true that she says: 'I was unacquainted with any of them. . . . I did not consider myself worthy to speak to them or strong enough to obey them';[70] but she also says: 'I was attracted to them by my knowledge of their method of life and prayer alone'[71]—a phrase of the utmost significance. At any rate, she very soon got into touch with them, for she was growing concerned about her experiences in mental prayer, which she feared might be delusions. 'It seemed to me,' she says in her downright way, 'that there must either be something very good about this or something terribly bad';[72] in either case, she felt that she needed expert direction. It is curious to reflect that the immediate cause of her consulting the Jesuit fathers was the belief of two other advisers that her 'trouble came from the devil' and that the Jesuits, being not only 'saintly,' but 'men of great experience in spiritual matters,'[73] would exorcize the intruder better than anyone else. With that somewhat bleak recommendation, and with all the secrecy that the nature of it made advisable, Teresa sent for a Father of the Society and gave him her full confidence. His verdict was the exact opposite of the other. She was clearly being led by the Holy Spirit; and she must on no account abandon mental prayer, but most 'work hard at it,' since the Lord was showing her special favours. She would be very much to blame if she failed to respond to His leading. How did she know that He was not desirous of using her to help others? (How indeed? she exclaims in parenthesis. 'It seems now that he was prophesying what the Lord afterwards did with me.')[74]

---

[70] L. XXIII (I, 146).
[71] *Ibid.*
[72] *Ibid.*
[73] L. XXIII (I, 151).
[74] L. XXIII (I, 151-2).

That interview marked the beginning of Teresa's new existence, and incidentally, too, of her devotion to the Society of Jesus. Thenceforward her prayer became, not an incident repeated so many times daily, but a part of the texture of her day, an element in her very being. Once upon a time, she had sought respite from devotion in outward things: now she could not concentrate upon these even when she would. 'The more I tried to think of other things, the more completely the Lord enveloped me in that sweetness and glory until I felt so completely surrounded by it that I could not flee from it in any direction.'[75] Disagreeable mortification, of a kind unimagined by the delicately-living nuns of the Incarnation, increased the austerity of her life, while further revelations of Our Lord increased her happiness. A month or two after her first contact with the Society, she met St. Francis Borgia, the former Duke of Gandía, who as a widower of forty had made a dramatic renunciation of wealth and position in order to enter it. St. Francis confirmed the judgment of her first Jesuit confessor, and advised her, if ever God should take possession of her spirit while she was engaged in meditation, not to attempt resistance.[76]

Shortly after this, St. Teresa had her first experience of rapture. Her confessor had been moved from Ávila, and his successor, whom she found equally helpful, had been talking to her about friendships of a certain type, which were lawful, but not expedient, and which she was unwilling to forego. Following his directions, she took the matter to God in prayer; and, while repeating the hymn *Veni, Creator*, she was seized with a transport 'so sudden that it almost carried me out of myself.'

> I could make no mistake about this, so clear was it. This was the first time that the Lord had granted me the favour of any kind of rapture. I heard these words: 'I will have thee converse now, not

[75] L. XXIV (I, 153).
[76] L. XXIV (I, 154).

> with men but with angels.' This simply amazed me, for my soul
> was greatly moved and the words were spoken to me in the depths
> of the spirit. For this reason they made me afraid, though on the
> other hand they brought me a great deal of comfort, which
> remained with me after the fear caused by the strangeness of the
> experiences had vanished.[77]

And, she observes, as she rounds off this chapter of her
autobiography, 'the words have come true.' Never from
that time was she able to make firm friends save of those
who, she believed, loved God and tried to serve Him.
She takes no credit for this: 'it has not been in my own
power to do so.'

> Unless I know that a person loves God or practises prayer, it is a
> real cross for me to have to do with him. I really believe this is
> the absolute truth.[78]

That seems a characteristically practical angle from
which to regard a supernatural favour.

II

AT ST. JOSEPH'S: TERESA OF JESUS
(1557–1562)

FOR some time after this first rapture, the chief incidents
in Teresa's exterior life were conflicts with her confessors.
Continually, in her books, she complains of the stupidity
of priests who, whatever their sanctity, are not well
enough educated to undertake the task of direction and
can only understand the progress of those who enjoy
experiences similar to their own. For us, whose opinion of
Spanish divines of that age has been formed by reading
such masters of the spiritual life as Osuna, Granada, Juan
de los Ángeles and St. John of the Cross, it is difficult to
realize how little was known of moral theology by even

[77] L. XXIV (I, 155).
[78] *Ibid.*

the Regular clergy. This becomes clear enough, however, from St. Teresa's narrative; and, though her reverence for the cloth forces her to remind us that these incompetent directors were all 'great servants of God,' and to attribute their apparent stupidity to the wiles of the devil, we are appalled to find how often, in the best of faith, they complacently called darkness light and light darkness.

Into the midst of Teresa's progress came a group of five or six such men—'all great servants of God'—who decided, on learning of her experiences, that she was suffering from diabolical delusions. She must reduce the amount of time spent in devotion, they told her; she must communicate less frequently; and she must cultivate distractions and shun solitude.[1]

So sure had Teresa been that she was on the right path at last that she could hardly believe her ears. Yet these men had both sanctity and learning; and her own confessor (though she afterwards found he was only testing her) was apparently taking their part. 'I had no one to talk to about it,' she sighs; 'they were all against me.'[2] For some two years she continued in this uncertain and nerve-racking state—'quite upset and worn out, with not the least idea what to do.'[3] No vision came to strengthen her, and her only comfort was found in some words which were borne into her consciousness one day when she was in a 'terrible state of exhaustion': 'Be not afraid, daughter, for it is I and I will not forsake thee: fear not.'[4]

Assurances of this nature were now granted to her with greater frequency and brought her an increasing inward peace. But the furnace had not tried her without effect and it is from this point onward that we can trace the emergence of her extraordinary virility. The natural

[1] L. XXV (I, 162).
[2] L. XXV (I, 162).
[3] L. XXV (I, 163).
[4] L. XXV (I, 164).

toughness of her rugged Castilian temperament is moulded by the Divine power into an irresistible strength. Without losing any of the engaging charm and friendliness which have distinguished her from girlhood, she develops a determination, a decisiveness, a fortitude which few women in history have possessed to a like degree. Much of this, so far as it appears in her writings, has in the past been obscured and diluted by the conventionality which is the refuge of so many translators. Let a passage which not even translation can spoil be quoted with all possible literalness to describe how Teresa's consciousness of God's all-powerful support could carry her through the fiercest temptations:

> 'Well, now,' I said to myself, 'if this Lord is so powerful, as I see He is, and know He is, and if the devils are His slaves (and of that there can be no doubt, for it is an article of the Faith), what harm can they do me, who am a servant of this Lord and King? How can I fail to have fortitude enough to fight against all hell?' So I took a cross in my hand and it really seemed that God was giving me courage: in a short time I found I was another person and I should not have been afraid to wrestle with devils, for with the aid of that cross I believed I could easily vanquish them all. . . . 'Come on, now, all of you,' I said. 'I am a servant of the Lord and I want to see what you can do to me.'
>
> It certainly seemed as if I had frightened all these devils, for I became quite calm and had no more fear of them. . . . They are no more trouble to me now than flies. They seem to me such cowards—as soon as they see that anyone despises them they have no strength left.[5]

Can that really have been written, we ask, by a woman in the sixteenth century?

Similar experiences—similar assurances and often similar voices—would come to her when she was troubled about other matters. Now she would be maligned and persecuted, and the Lord would put to her the simple question: 'Why dost thou fear?' And 'even at that time,' she records, 'I began at once to feel strong.'[6] Now a confessor would give her advice which she was doubtful

[5] L. XXV (I, 164–5).
[6] L. XXVI (I, 167).

about accepting; and the Lord would still her doubts by telling her to obey him.[7] Now authority forbade her to read certain books which had given her pleasure, and the Lord said: 'Be not distressed, for I will give thee a living book.'[8] By narrating such simple incidents as these she shows us how she was gradually building up the fortitude of which she would have such need in the years to come.

It was perhaps in 1558 (if 'at the end of two years' means two years after her first encounter with the Jesuit) that Teresa experienced her first intellectual vision.[9] 'I saw Christ at my side,' she declares, 'or, to put it better, I was conscious of Him, for neither with the eyes of the body nor with those of the soul did I see anything.'[10] She finds this experience impossible to describe except by means of analogies and comparisons, which extend to many pages. At first, never having heard of such a thing, she was afraid and 'did nothing but weep'; but, 'as soon as He addressed a single word to me to reassure me, I became quiet again, as I had been before, and was quite happy and free from fear.'[11]

Another of her well-known visions was an imaginary one of Christ in His Resurrection Body, 'in very great beauty and majesty,' a type of vision which, 'even in its whiteness and radiance alone ... exceeds all that we can imagine.'[12] The passage in which she glosses this descrip-

---

[7] L. XXVI (I, 168).
[8] *Ibid.*
[9] There are three kinds of vision (in ascending order of perfection, says St. Teresa—L. XXVIII: C.W. I, 179). (i) Corporeal, manifested to the bodily eye; (ii) Imaginary, *i.e.* representation by the action of the imagination alone, without the intervention of the eye; (iii) Intellectual, i.e. perception by the understanding without the production of any sensible image ('neither with the eyes of the body nor with those of the soul,' L. XXVII: C.W. I, 170). St. Teresa (R. IV: C.W. I, 320) never had a corporeal vision. Locutions, *mutatis mutandis*, are similarly classified.
[10] L. XXVII (I, 170).
[11] *Ibid.*
[12] L. XXVIII (I, 179–80).

tion is worth quoting as an example of her style: though entirely untrained, she was, as we shall see, a natural artist of the first order, and it is difficult to believe that these lines were written without being carefully revised and polished:

> It is not a radiance which dazzles, but a soft whiteness and an infused radiance which, without wearying the eyes, causes them the greatest delight; nor are they wearied by the brightness which they see in seeing this Divine beauty. So different from any earthly light is the brightness and light now revealed to the eyes that, by comparison with it, the brightness of our sun seems dim. . . . It is as if we were to look at a very clear stream, in a bed of crystal, reflecting the sun's rays, and then to see a very muddy stream, in an earthy bed and overshadowed by clouds. Not that the sun, or any other such light, enters into the vision: on the contrary, it is like a natural light and all other kinds of light seem artificial. It is a light which never gives place to night, and, being always light, is disturbed by nothing. It is of such a kind, indeed, that no one, however powerful his intellect, could, in the whole course of his life, imagine it as it is.[13]

And now Teresa began to receive constant visions of Christ in His Resurrection Body or on the Cross. Once, when she was holding the cross of her rosary, it seemed to her that He put out His hand—

> and took it from me, and, when He gave it back to me, it had become four large stones, much more precious than diamonds. . . . On the cross, with exquisite workmanship, were portrayed the five wounds. He told me that henceforward it would always look to me like that, and so it did: I could never see the wood of which it was made, but only these stones. To nobody, however, did it look like this except to myself.[14]

But the most famous of her supernatural experiences, and one of the best known of such phenomena in Christian history, is the vision generally termed the Transverberation of her heart. This we can date, with comparative confidence, in the year 1559. It was not, as is generally supposed, a single vision, but one which was

[13] L. XXVIII (I, 180).
[14] L. XXIX (I, 189–90).

repeated several times over a period of days. She would see, close beside her, on her left hand, the bodily form of an angel. The vision was of a type which she seldom experienced, but it was of unusual clarity. The angel 'was not tall, but short, and very beautiful, his face so aflame that he appeared to be one of the highest types of angel who seem to be all afire. They must be those who are called cherubim.' In his hand was a long golden spear with a tip of red-hot iron. Then came the extraordinary and characteristic part of the vision. Time after time the angel's spear seemed to pierce her heart, and penetrate to her very entrails, causing her pain so sharp as to make her moan. The pain was not physical (though the body participated in it), but spiritual, and caused her 'greater bliss than any that can come from the whole of creation.' 'So excessive,' she adds, 'was the sweetness caused me by this intense pain that one can never wish to lose it, nor will one's soul be content with anything less than God.'[15]

'During the days that this continued,' the account goes on, 'I went about as if in a stupor. I had no wish to see or speak with anyone, but only to hug my pain.'[16] It hardly seems possible that these are the words of Teresa the foundress, the woman of affairs, the writer of those hundreds of intensely practical letters. But genuine visionaries, as students of the subject know, are nearly always the most practical people imaginable, and St. Teresa is not the first to have come down from the mountain of supernatural experience and mingled with the animated crowds in the busy plain. At the time of the Transverberation, though she could not have known it, she was nearing the end of the quarter-century during which she had been an obscure daughter of Carmel and standing on the threshold of the life-work which was to make her immortal. As for confessor she now had another and a famous Jesuit, who figures in the later history of

[15] L. XXIX (I, 192–3).
[16] L. XXIX (I, 193).

Spanish mysticism, P. Baltasar Álvarez. And almost at the same time as she came to know him, she made the acquaintance of an even more remarkable man, who can hardly have failed to influence her future actions, and may even, under God, have been their chief inspiration.

St. Peter of Alcántara was an elderly Franciscan friar from Extremadura, known as a preacher, as a devout solitary and (in St. Teresa's phrase) as the author of some 'little books on prayer,'[17] but principally, within his own Order, as a fervid follower of the Discalced Reform. At the end of the preceding century a number of Franciscans had decided to live according to a stricter Rule than was then in vogue, with the aim of restoring the simplicity of life which had been the practice of their founder. In the year of St. Teresa's birth, when he was only sixteen, St. Peter joined the Discalced Reform (the adjective, of course, indicates that the members of the Reform went unshod), and from then to the time of his death, in 1562, he lived a life of the most extreme austerity.

Precisely when he met St. Teresa we do not know, but it must have been around 1559,[18] when he visited Ávila as Commissary-General of the Discalced Franciscans. A widowed lady, Doña Guiomar de Ulloa, to whom she had confided her experiences with unintelligent confessors, thought that the two would have much in common; so she obtained permission for Teresa to stay with her for a week and thus arranged for her to meet Fray Peter. The first impression he seems to have made upon her was one of extreme old age (though he was barely sixty) and of extreme asceticism. For forty years he had slept for only

---

[17] L. XXX (I, 194). On St. Peter of Alcántara, see *Studies*, II, 99–120.

[18] St. Teresa describes him as Commissary-General of the Custody of St. Joseph (L. XXX: I, 197) and it was in 1559 that he was appointed to this office.

an hour and a half nightly, seated, with his head resting
against a piece of wood fixed to the wall, in a cell four
and a half feet long. During all these years, 'however hot
the sun or heavy the rain, he never wore his hood, or
anything on his feet, and his only dress was a habit of
sackcloth ... It was a very common thing for him to
take food only once in three days.' No wonder he looked
to Teresa 'so extremely weak that he seemed to be made
of nothing but roots of trees.'[19]

A rather terrifying person, in short, especially as,
'except when answering questions,' he was 'a man of
few words.' And yet, as she charmingly adds, 'with all
this holiness he was very affable,' and, 'when he did
speak it was a delight to listen to him, for he was
extremely intelligent.'[20]

The two had 'many talks' together;[21] and at first, it
seems, Teresa did most of the talking. She told him all
she could think of about her spiritual life, and in particular her experiences of mental prayer, and to her great
gratification discovered that, 'almost from the beginning,' he understood them and could interpret them to
her. Like her Jesuit directors, he was 'quite certain that
it was the work of the Spirit.'[22] But after that the silent
old friar seems to have unburdened himself also, telling
her 'about his own affairs and undertakings.' He saw
that she was entertaining 'desires which he himself had
already carried into effect';[23] and, although the context
of that phrase has reference to the interior life, it seems
likely that the phrase itself means that she had projected
a reform of her own Order and discussed it with him in
detail. Before parting, they arranged to write to each
other, which they did until St. Peter's death.

[19] L. XXVII (I, 176–7).
[20] L. XXVII (I, 177).
[21] L. XXX (I, 195).
[22] *Ibid.*
[23] L. XXX (I, 196).

That the project of founding a reformed house of her Order had been in St. Teresa's mind before St. Peter of Alcántara's visit cannot for a moment be doubted. If we can trust her own chronology (which, it must be confessed, is by no means faultless) discussions 'about the foundation in Ávila of the first convent for Discalced nuns' had begun in 1558,[24] and there are indications that the idea had been in her mind quite four years earlier. Whenever she may first have conceived it, she had soon thought it out in great detail. Her original desire, which we have seen growing in her from the time of her second conversion, was to follow her own vocation by keeping her Rule 'with the greatest possible perfection.'[25] At this time, throughout the whole Order, the Rule was observed according to a Bull of Mitigation granted it in 1432; and at the Incarnation the further relaxations, the comforts and the privileges which were allowed seemed to Teresa clean contrary to the principle of holy poverty.

One day, in the course of a conversation with others, a young cousin of hers, María de Ocampo, at that time a boarding-pupil at the Incarnation, asked her why she did not initiate a Discalced Reform among the Carmelites: 'it would be quite possible,' she said, 'to find a way of establishing a convent.'[26] The suggestion may not perhaps have been meant very seriously, but it fell in so well with ideas which had been in her own mind that she discussed it with Doña Guiomar, who was becoming more and more interested in her. Together they came to a very definite conclusion. The project was an excellent one, but the endowment even of one small community would be beyond the means of either Doña Guiomar or the enthusiastic and generously disposed María. Besides, being very happy at the Incarnation, Teresa shrank from taking

[24] R. IV (I, 319–20): 'Some eighteen years ago'—and she was writing in 1576.
[25] L. XXXII (I, 218).
[26] L. XXXII (I, 219: see also n. 4).

so irrevocable a step as leaving it. After all, she was forty-five; and she had spent her entire life as a simple nun, always following and never once leading. She must surely be too much inured to the beaten track to take the lead now.

But one day, after Communion, she received a command from the Lord Himself which altered the whole matter. For by this time she had trained herself, not only to follow her superiors, but to listen for, and obey, the voice of God. And there could be no mistake about what she heard now: the Lord made her 'wonderful promises' and gave her 'the most explicit commands' to work for this aim 'with all her might.'[27] He even gave the convent-to-be the name by which it was to become famous— St. Joseph's—and ended by charging Teresa to tell her confessor this, and to say 'that it was He Who was giving her this command and that He asked him not to oppose it or to hinder her in carrying it out.'[28]

From first to last, Teresa, like all good Castilians, was a realist; and even her loyalty to her Master never blinded her to the probable cost of obeying Him. She had thought and talked of her project, without 'any great degree of determination or certainty that the thing would be done'; and she found that it looked very different when the moment came for translating in into action. The task seemed to her a 'great burden'; so revolutionary a move, especially when made by a woman, would certainly cause 'serious disturbances.'[29] There would be a practical difficulty—lack of resources. There would be difficulties with the local authorities; for every town, in those days, had to find means of checking the increase of religious houses, which sprang up like mushrooms and could so easily become a drain on the municipality. There would be difficulties within the Order: not everybody

[27] L. XXXII (I, 219: see also n. 4).
[28] L. XXXII (I, 220).
[29] *Ibid.*

wants to be reformed and those who do not are apt to say so with some vigour.

Teresa's confessor, P. Álvarez, when consulted about the idea, was not unsympathetic, 'but he saw that, humanly speaking, there was no way of putting it into practice.' It may be doubted, in fact, if the Reform would ever have been accomplished had not the Lord appeared to Teresa and spoken of it 'again and again.' She took a good deal of convincing; but 'so numerous were the motives and arguments' which He put before her that she had no choice but to yield.[30]

So the matter was taken to Teresa's own Superior, and then to the Provincial, who carried it one stage farther by promising his sanction. But as soon as the proposal became generally known it met with a storm of opposition. 'There descended upon us a persecution so severe that it is impossible in a few words to describe it.'[31] And nowhere, as might have been expected, was the opposition so strong as at the Incarnation. That one can well understand: the fine ladies who lived so delicately would hardly want a house of their own Order with an austere Rule planted at their very doorstep. Teresa became highly unpopular.

> The nuns said I was insulting them; that there were others there who were better than myself, and so I could serve God quite well where I was; that I had no love for my own convent; and that I should have done better to get money for that than for founding another. Some said I ought to be thrown into the prison-cell.[32]

So loud was the clamour that, although a house had been found and the deeds were ready for signature, the Provincial went back on his promise and refused his consent: quite apart from the opposition, he said, there was too little money and even that little was not assured.

[30] *Ibid.*
[31] L. XXXII (I, 221).
[32] L. XXXIII (I, 224).

This *volte-face* destroyed the one argument with which Teresa could publicly justify her action: if the Provincial said, 'No,' then, notwithstanding her visions and voices, she could not possibly go farther.

Her position now was certainly unenviable. Against her were the prohibition of the Provincial, the belief of her confessor that she had been deluded, the enhanced ridicule of the people in general and the anger of her own sisters. The one fact which might have carried conviction she did not, for obvious reasons, feel free to divulge—namely, that she was acting in obedience to her Lord's direct command.

But see with what repose and dignity she bore all this. 'It seemed to me that I had done all I possibly could. . . . So I remained in my own house, quite content and happy.'[33] 'Content and happy,' with her sisters pointing at her and speaking ill of her; because within the convent she had her own cell, and within her soul she had her interior castle. There she stayed, 'content and happy'; and, while scandal and gossip raged without, her spiritual life grew. After a time, rumours got about that she had been 'seeing things'; and her friends came to her 'in great concern to say that these were bad times,' and she might be denounced to the Inquisition.[34] And what did this extraordinary woman say to that? Why, she laughed at the idea. No supercilious serenity about this saint; not even an enigmatic smile; but a good ringing laugh. For her conscience was clear and her mind at ease.

> So I told them not to be afraid, for my soul would be in a very bad way if there were anything about it which could make me fear the Inquisition. If ever I thought there might be, I would go and pay it a visit of my own accord; and if anything were alleged against me the Lord would deliver me and I should be very much the gainer.[35]

[33] *Ibid.*
[34] L. XXXIII (I, 225).
[35] L. XXXIII (I, 226).

For 'five or six months' Teresa remained in her self-chosen retirement. The project was to all appearances abandoned, and, strange to relate, the Lord gave her 'not a single command.' And yet she 'could not get rid of her belief that the foundation would be duly made,' as in fact it very soon was.

Once more Teresa found helpers in the Society of Jesus. In April 1561, a new Rector, P. Gaspar de Salazar, was apointed to its Avilan house—'a very spiritual man, of great courage, intelligence and learning.'[36] He became her Director—the most sympathetic she had till then had —and, as soon as he heard of her plans for the Reform, he gave her his unqualified support. This time, made wiser by experience, she determined, if she could, to cut out the backbiting and the commotion by going to work secretly, and asking for the Provincial's permission only when the arrangements had been provisionally made. So in August 1561, after collecting some money 'from various sources,' she arranged for her own sister, Doña Juana de Ahumada, to buy and furnish the house, as if for herself. It was too small for a convent, even though she had long since decided to limit her numbers to thirteen, but it was all she could afford, so she furnished it as well as she could and wondered what to do next.[37]

Her great fear was that one of the few people who had had to be let into the secret 'would say something about it to the Provincial... in which case all would be up with it.'[38] However, it so happened that a wealthy Toledan lady, recently widowed, Doña Luisa de la Cerda, had asked his special permission for Teresa to visit her, and, not without apprehension at what may easily have been her first long journey, she went to stay with her for the first six months of 1562. Despite misgivings at the prospect of living in a wealthy household, she soon grew

---

[36] L. XXXIII (I, 226–7).
[37] L. XXXIII (I, 228–9).
[38] L. XXXIV (I, 232).

very intimate with Doña Luisa, and no part of her *Life* is more charming than the passage in which she describes that visit.[39] While she was there, she made the acquaintance of another lady who had conceived the idea of founding a Carmelite convent and who had in fact obtained the necessary patent from Rome.[40] From this lady she learned for the first time that the original Carmelite Rule forbade religious houses to have any possessions—that is to say, any regular income. This new idea quickly took root in her mind and quickened her desire to complete her foundation on that basis. Why, after all, did it need any money of its own? Why should it not trust for its income to God?

So she consulted various people, including her confessor, on the practicability of founding a convent in complete poverty. None of them would entertain the idea for a moment. One Dominican friar to whom she wrote 'answered me in a letter two sheets long, full of refutations and theology; in this he told me that he had made a close study of the subject and tried to dissuade me from my project.' Teresa replied, with a tartness unusual in her, 'that I had no wish to make use of theology and should not thank him for his learning in this matter if it was going to keep me from following my vocation, from being true to the vow of poverty that I had made, and from observing Christ's precepts with due perfection.'[41] Only one of her advisers appears to have agreed with her: a man who had lived with poverty till he knew it as an intimate friend—St. Peter of Alcántara. When she found that she had his support, she sought no other. Finally, renewed visions, which she had again begun to experience on deciding to make the foundation, culminated in a 'deep rapture,' during which

[39] L. XXXIV (I, 233–4). The passage is referred to further on p. 52, below.
[40] L. XXXV (I, 241–2).
[41] L. XXXV (I, 243).

the Lord told me that I must on no account fail to found the convent in poverty, for that was His Father's will, and His own will, and He would help me.[42]

In July, 1562, with her Provincial's consent, Teresa decided to return to Ávila, where a new Prioress was about to be elected at the Incarnation. Her dignified policy of silence, followed by her absence in Toledo, had brought about a reaction in her favour, and she had reason to believe that she might be the person elected— obviously a contingency to be avoided if she was about to found the first house of her Reform. So, to the great regret of Doña Luisa, she set out, to arrive after a weary journey over the hot and parched plain, at a most auspicious moment. For awaiting her were, not only the Bishop and St. Peter of Alcántara, but the Brief and patent for the foundation of the new Convent, which had been secretly applied for, from Rome.[43]

It now remained only to obtain local sanction, which St. Peter and his Avilan host effected by talking over the Bishop. This was no easy matter. When St. Peter had reached Ávila, the Bishop had been away in a neighbouring village. There the 'saintly old man' tracked him down, to find that he was completely opposed to the foundation of a new convent without endowments. But he persuaded him to return to Ávila and discuss the matter with St. Teresa, and, when she had importuned him, he gave way, though only because 'he was so much drawn to people whom he saw determined to serve the Lord.'[44]

So, with 'the full weight of authority,' but yet amid the greatest secrecy, so as not to risk a general disclosure, Teresa's first foundation was made on St. Bartholomew's Day (August 24), 1562. It so happened that she had been granted leave of absence from the Incarnation to nurse a sick brother-in-law during his wife's absence from home,

[42] *Ibid.*
[43] L. XXXVI (I, 248).
[44] *Ibid.*

and was thus able herself to give the habit of the Reform to those first four nuns who, in their new garb of coarsest frieze, were her very own. Her joy, when the foundation was made, the bell hung, the statues of Our Lady and St. Joseph installed above the entrance, and the first nuns received, knew no bounds:

> It was like being in Heaven to me to see the Most Holy Sacrament reserved, and to find ourselves supporting four poor orphans (for they were taken without dowries).... From the very beginning we tried to receive only persons whose examples might serve as a foundation on which we could effectively build up our plan of a community of great perfection, given to prayer, and carry out a work which I believed would lead to the Lord's service and honour the habit of His glorious Mother. It was for this that I yearned. It was also a great comfort to me that I had done what the Lord had so often commanded me and that there was one more church here than there had previously been, dedicated to my glorious Father Saint Joseph.... I was so happy, therefore, that I was quite carried away by the intensity of my prayer.[45]

But hardly was the ceremony over than Teresa was tortured by renewed misgivings. Previously, she seems almost to have forgotten that she was acting against the command of her Provincial, as though the sanction of the Ordinary absolved her from disregarding it. Certainly, she admits, it had occurred to her that the placing of the convent under the jurisdiction of the Ordinary might cause him displeasure, but she had also hoped, on what grounds is not clear, 'that he might not trouble about it.'[46] Now she realized that she would have to face his possible censure; and with the fear of that came a host of other fears as well. Would the slender foundation hold? Would the nuns endure the strictness of the Rule? Would food be found for them? Would she herself take kindly to so mean a dwelling after living in a 'large, pleasant house' for twenty-five years?[47]

[45] L. XXXVI (I, 250).
[46] L. XXXVI (I, 251).
[47] *Ibid.*

So heavily did these thoughts weigh upon her that they plunged her into the depths of depression. 'Here I was,' she reflects, 'such a short time ago, thinking that I would not exchange my happiness with anyone on earth, and now the very cause of it was tormenting me so sorely that I did not know what to do with myself.'[48] There followed a long interior conflict, in which at length the Saint's courage triumphed, and, kneeling before the Blessed Sacrament, she promised to seek permission to enter the new house herself, and, if she could do so with a good conscience, to take a vow of enclosure. The moment this was done, she says, 'the devil fled, leaving me quiet and happy, and I remained so and have been so ever since. . . . So great is my happiness that I sometimes wonder what earthly choice I could possibly have made which would have been more delightful.'[49]

Hardly had St. Teresa returned to the Incarnation than the troubles she had foreseen began. Her secret was out. The new Prioress, elected only a fortnight before, sent for her and heard her story by no means unsympathetically, but decided that it must be repeated to the Provincial. He, quite naturally, reprimanded her, but at a subsequent interview proved surprisingly tractable and promised that, once the commotion in the city had subsided, she should go to live at St. Joseph's.

But the commotion had broken out again with renewed fury. Both the City Council and the Cathedral Chapter insisted that the house should at once be closed. A joint conference between them and representatives of the Orders established in Ávila concurred in this decision almost unanimously. It was questioned only by a young Dominican, Fray Domingo Báñez, who later had a great deal to do with St. Teresa and became very proud of the stand he had made. The conference led nowhere, as the Provincial refused to take action; and eventually legal

[48] *Ibid.*
[49] L. XXXVI (I, 252).

proceedings were instituted before the Royal Council. At one point Teresa's opponents were inclined to come to terms provided the house were properly endowed, and to this, but for her voices, she would probably have agreed. A vision of St. Peter of Alcántara, who had recently died, confirmed her determination not to yield, and she thereupon indicated that the lawsuit must continue.[50]

For two full years—from August 1562 to August 1564—the dispute dragged on. Inch by inch Teresa gained her ground. About March 1563 the Provincial permitted her provisionally to transfer to St. Joseph's with some of her companions from the Incarnation. Soon after this, more joined it, alms increased and public opinion began to veer in the Discalced's favour. On August 22, the provisional permission to transfer was made official, and, exactly twelve months later, was confirmed by the Papal Nuncio. Only with that last act did opposition disappear and the lawsuit was abandoned.[51]

So the lady-nun of the Incarnation, Doña Teresa de Cepeda y Ahumada, became the 'little nun of St. Joseph's' the *indigna sierva* of all, Teresa de Jesús. And for four and a half years—until the summer of 1567—she lived at St. Joseph's, which soon attained its full complement of thirteen. 'Those were the most restful years of my life,' she wrote in 1573, 'the calm and quiet of which my soul often sorely misses.'[52] For the first time completely enclosed, she had more time for mental prayer, for thought about the development of the Discalced Reform and for her earliest attempts at writing. During this period she revised and completed one large book,[53] began a second and was ordered by her confessor to write a third.[54] But, despite these achievements, the sojourn at

[50] L. XXXVI (I, 254–7).
[51] L. XXXVI (I, 259).
[52] F. I (III, 1).
[53] The *Life*, of which the first draft was finished in June 1562 and a second and enlarged one at about the end of 1565.
[54] F. Prologue (III, xxii).

St. Joseph's, by comparison with the strenuous fifteen years that were to follow, was pre-eminently a period of tranquillity and contemplation. Turning over the final pages of the *Life*, one seems to see its author, a woman of fifty, standing alone upon that stage, for so long crowded with the characters of her trivial drama, but now at last quite empty. Slowly, it would seem, the curtain is falling, and her active life, instead of being just about to begin, is ended. Perhaps she, too, was feeling like that as she penned the lines which follow as the epilogue to an obscure career which had ended with a brief blaze of undesired publicity:

> As I am now out of the world, and my companions are few and saintly, I look down upon the world as from above and care very little what people say or what is known about me. I care more about the smallest degree of progress achieved by one single soul than for all that people may say about me; for, since I have been here, it has been the Lord's will that this should become the aim of all my desires. He has given me a life which is a kind of sleep; when I see things I nearly always seem to be dreaming them. In myself I find no great propensity either to joy or to sorrow. If anything produces either of these conditions in me, it passes so quickly that I marvel and the feeling it leaves is like the feeling left by a dream.[55]

'It is thus, dear sir and father,' she adds to her confessor, 'that I live now. Your Reverence must beseech God either to take me to be with Him or to give me the means of serving Him.'[56] We cannot tell which of these prayers his Reverence thought the more fitting. Perhaps Teresa, fatigued by her recent conflicts, expected an answer to the first of them; but it came, as we shall see, to the second. Far from drawing to its close, her active life was only just unfolding. Had she died in 1567, she would have been forgotten save in the annals of Carmel; but she lived fifteen years longer and her name is known in every corner of the Christian world.

[55] L. XL (I, 298).
[56] *Ibid.*

PART TWO

ACHIEVEMENT

III

THE *LIFE*: A 'BOOK OF THE MERCIES OF GOD'
(1562–1565)

St. Teresa's autobiography, the chief source for the two foregoing chapters, covers her outward and inward life down to June 1562. To some scholarly and sensitive critics, including her latest Spanish editor, P. Silverio,[1] it is her masterpiece—a view which I cannot myself share. I find in it—as every reader must—innate talent of a very high order: vividness of description, flexibility of expression, a captivating freshness, an earnestness and a devotion which in their moments of greatest intensity are irresistible. But though, from the literary point of view, the book is amazingly mature for one who had written nothing previously, it is inferior in this respect to the *Interior Castle*, which, too, for sheer beauty, and for the number and quality of its purple patches, must take the first place. Even more marked is its superiority over the *Life* as regards maturity of experience and devotion, which, together with its white-hot ardour, marks it out as one of the greatest mystical works in Christian literature. The *Life* must be relegated to a lower level than this, though its place is still very high. What we can say about it without fear of contradiction is that it is fundamental;

[1] C.W. I, 2.

that it gives us the background of St. Teresa's life and an insight into her character which can be gained in no other way; that no one can be said to know her who is not familiar with it.

Its defects—if defects they are: one often feels that they bring the author nearer to us and make her work the more human—are mainly of proportion and construction, and to some extent these may be explained by the way in which the book was written. There were at least two drafts of it; and there may have been more. Not long after her second conversion (c. 1556–7), for example, Teresa was searching for words in which to describe her spiritual experiences and found them in an ardent little treatise by a Spanish Franciscan, Bernardino de Laredo, the *Ascent of Mount Sion*.[2] As this gave an accurate description of her symptoms, she 'marked the relevant passages' and showed them to a layman who was advising her, and to a priest friend of his, 'together with the best general account of my life and sins that I could.'[3] Hoornaert believes that this was a written account—'the first document of her spiritual state, but it no longer exists.'[4] I see no reason to suppose that it ever did exist: Teresa describes the account as 'not being given [*hecha relación*] in confession, as he was a layman';[5] and this way of putting it suggests an oral, not a written, story. At the same time, it would seem impossible that one who wrote so readily, whose first published book shows such maturity, and who, as we know, was practising such intense introspection can have failed to have set down her experiences, again and again, in writing, and there can be little doubt that parts of the 'spiritual relations' in the *Life* were written long before the rest.

It may not have been long after 1557, indeed, that she

2 For an account of Laredo and his book, see *Studies*, II, 41–76.
3 C.W. I, 149–50.
4 *St. Teresa in Her Writings*, London, 1931, p. 217.
5 C.W. I, 150.

conceived the idea of writing her autobiography and actually set to work upon it. Though written at the command of her confessor, we cannot say exactly when this command was given. Báñez, the sole champion of her Reform at the joint meeting in Ávila, later deposed: 'She had written this book when I first came into contact with her and she wrote it with the leave (*sic*) of her previous confessors.'[6] The last phrase suggests a process which had been going on for some time, and I cannot help thinking that the little company of intimate spiritual friends, described in Chapter XVI of the *Life* as 'we five,'[7] could have told us something of that book's origins.

By 1562, a draft of the book was completed: the latter part of it, or perhaps the greater part, had been written at Doña Luisa's in Toledo. Apparently it was approved, for later in the same year, when she was back at St. Joseph's, Ávila, her new confessor—like the first, and like P. Báñez, a Dominican—told her to bring it up to date. Further encouragement came from various sources: from 'other confessors who had given her the same command', from 'many of her friends,' and (not least in importance) from an Inquisitor whom she had met at Ávila.[8] Not only were the final chapters of the book now written, but the earlier part was revised and enlarged as well. All this work was done in the tranquillity of St. Joseph's, but exactly when we cannot say. A number of allusions in the book itself suggest that little or no progress was made with it for nearly two years, and that in its final form it was completed in the latter part of 1565—perhaps even at the very end of that year, or early in the year following.[9]

Neither this nor any other book of St. Teresa's was written for publication; and, when completed, the manuscript went about on journeys more perilous even than

[6] C.W. I, 2.
[7] L. XVI (I, 99).
[8] The testimony here is Gracián's (C.W. I, 3).
[9] These matters are discussed in C.W. I, 3–5.

those soon to be made by its author—journeys which we may be thankful that it ever survived. It had to be examined and approved by this confessor and by that, and before long copies of it were being made. P. Báñez, who had now become St. Teresa's firm friend, began to reproach her for sending it about too freely. He realized, however, that 'the fault was not hers,'[10] and indeed she had often no say in the matter. What harm could be done in those days by giving publicity to a piece of intimate writing may be gathered from an episode relating to an imperious 'great lady,' the Princess of Éboli, of whom we shall learn more hereafter. Hearing of the book about four years after its completion, she insisted upon its being lent to her, promising Teresa that it should be read only by herself and her husband. The Princess being (at that time) a good friend of the Reform, it was hardly politic to refuse her. But her undertaking was not kept: the book's contents became the property of the entire household; and some of the experiences it describes were scoffed at as delusions.

Within a short time, it was denounced to the Inquisition and the ever-watchful Báñez quickly read through the manuscript, and, after making a few slight emendations, took it to the Inquisitors himself. Their judgment being entirely favourable, Teresa left it for safety in their hands, until she thought well to have it copied for her Reformed foundations: one of the first of these copies was made by the loving hand of her niece Teresita. Both this copy and the venerable original can now be seen in the grand old library of El Escorial.

Although it tells us so much about her external life, St. Teresa's book is essentially a spiritual autobiography, and there is great significance in an alternative title by which she used to refer to it. 'As you see,' she wrote to a correspondent shortly before her death, 'I am not in hell, which I have long since deserved to be. It was for that

[10] C.W. I, 6

reason that I entitled the book "Of the Mercies of God."[11]

Three strands are woven into its texture: the exterior life, the interior life, and objective spiritual teaching. First come ten chapters which are autobiographical in the usual sense of that word, taking us from Teresa's birth to the time of her second conversion. Then follows a huge digression of twelve chapters, forming a self-contained treatise on mental prayer as St. Teresa then knew it and embodying the well-known figure of the Four Waters. Chapter XXIII begins, 'I will now return to the place where I left off the description of my life,'[12] and picks up the external narrative again at the place where the author comes into contact with the Society of Jesus; but after a few pages she is digressing again—this time into a generalization on locutions, which continues as far as Chapter XXVIII. This begins: 'Returning to our subject. . . .'[13] Now the emphasis is on the interior life, and remains there for five chapters—to the end, so far as we can tell, of the first draft. Of the remaining eight chapters, which form the material subsequently added, the main theme is the foundation of St. Joseph's, Ávila, but here the exterior and the interior life are balanced more evenly than in any other part of the book, and it is on the interior note, in a passage already quoted, that the book ends.[14]

Of the external autobiography the first two chapters of this study have given some idea and we shall look at the objective treatise on mental prayer almost immediately. But first, in a few lines, let us deal with the spiritual autobiography—not in any way summarily or exhaustively, for it is so rich in experience that no summary can possibly serve as an alternative to reading it, but in order to extract from it a few traits which may add more detail to our picture of its author.

[11] LL. 388 (November 9, 1581).
[12] C.W. I, 145.
[13] C.W. I, 178.
[14] P. 45, above.

One of the happiest of these is its solicitude for the beginner—a trait which we also find, perhaps more surprisingly, in St. John of the Cross. So much does St. Teresa tell us of her own early life, and so ruthlessly does she lay bare her own imperfections, that we should expect her to have a true mother's thought for the weakest of her children. She is always 'most profitable for beginners.'[15] It takes her longer to describe the first stage of the contemplative life than the second and the third put together. She can enter into the difficulties and the trials of the spiritually immature, and, like an understanding physician, she can administer the very best of consolations —the reminder that she has suffered from them herself: 'I endured them for many years; and, when I was able to draw but one drop of water from this blessed well, I used to think that God was granting me a favour. I know how grievous such trials are and I think they need more courage than do many others in the world.'[16]

She is also aware of the beginner's pitfalls. One of these is his tendency to attempt too much and to imagine that his very ordinary experiences are transcendental. Another is depression at having no conscious devotion—or, as we commonly put it, at not 'feeling good.' Connected with this is the habit of setting overmuch store on sensible devotion, sometimes described by the mystics as 'spiritual consolations' or 'sweetness in prayer.'

> Mild feelings of devotion which ... issue in tears and other brief emotional outlets are merely frail flowerets blasted at the first breath of persecution: they are a good beginning, and the emotions they engender are holy ones, but I do not call them true devotion at all.[17]
>
> We must not show ourselves to be striving after spiritual consolations; come what may, the great thing for us to do is to embrace the Cross.[18]

[15] L. XI (I, 62).
[16] L. XI (I, 67).
[17] L. XXV (I, 160).
[18] L. XXII (I, 141).

In those last words we touch the hard core of St. Teresa's spiritual virility. That is one reason why she is such salutary reading—and not only for beginners. A closely allied reason is her common-sense. When we make minor allowances for the age and the country in which she lived—both very different from our own—we find her amazingly modern. And accompanying her modernity is an unflinching realism tempered by a strong sense of humour. To put it in another way, hers is a perfectly balanced personality with its centre both firm and true.

She had a keen devotional sense, for example, but that does not mean that she approves of all types of devotion. On the contrary:

> From foolish devotions may God deliver us.[19]

She has a great reverence for 'men of prayer, leading the religious life,' but when she sees them standing on their absurd dignity and 'making a great fuss about niceties concerning their honour'—well, she just 'enjoys a quiet laugh.'[20] She has been brought up to show proper respect to the well-born and highly placed—though she is not afraid, where necessary, to speak her mind to them—but as soon as she went to stay with a 'great lady,' who, she had always understood, was to be envied, her innate common-sense, quite proof against conventional notions, showed her that this was not so:

> I learned that people of rank have to be careful to behave according to their state, which hardly allows them to live.... Often the very food which they eat has more to do with their position than with their liking.... God deliver me from this sinful fuss....
>
> Then, with regard to servants, though hers were good, one can really place very little trust in them. It is impossible to talk more to one of them than to another; otherwise the favoured one is disliked by the rest. This is slavery.[21]

[19] L. XIII (I, 80).
[20] L. XXI (I, 134).
[21] L. XXXIV (I, 234).

It is as well to establish one fact before we look at more of St. Teresa's work, or read any of it for ourselves—that she is a thoroughly safe and trustworthy guide, who can be relied upon not to lead one astray.

Again, the *Life* begins to show us something of her relations with God. The successive stages of her life of prayer were the stages of a growing intimacy with God; and, because she was in fact intimate with Him, she spoke intimately to Him, and then, writing simply and naturally, as she always did, she reproduced parts of those conversations for the benefit of others. In the Spanish she uses the most colloquial language here, which, in translating it, I have tried to free from the shackles of conventional piety:

> Often I beseech the Lord, if He must upset me so much, to let me be free from it at times like these. 'My God,' I say to Him sometimes, 'when shall my soul be wholly employed in Thy praise, instead of being torn to pieces in this way, and quite helpless?'[22]

In one place she refers touchingly to 'that silly way in which I often speak to Him without knowing what I am saying; for it is love that speaks.'[23] But that directness conveys a strong sense of the immediacy of Teresa's contact with her God. The same effect is produced on the reader by many of her accounts of her locutions and visions. It is because her definitions and descriptions are clearly and simply phrased and based on genuine experience that they have become classical, and that, in particular, on the distinctions between different types of locution and vision, she is accepted, for all her disclaimers of learning, as an authority.

In what is only a simple biographical sketch, and not a treatise, I do not insist further on this, but it is so outstanding a characteristic of the *Life* that it must be mentioned even here. Strange that the author of such a book, having written it on the instructions of her confessors, and

[22] L. XVII (I, 103).
[23] L. XXXIV (I, 235).

for their benefit alone, should have quite expected that the Father to whom she sent it to read would burn it, and, acquiescing in whatever his decision might be, merely have added: 'I should prefer it not to be burned, however, before it has been seen by the three persons, known to Your Reverence, who are or have been my confessors.'[24] Fortunately it was spared, both by the confessor and by the Inquisition, to become one of the best loved autobiographies ever written.

It is on those things that St. Teresa's own daughters, and others who go to her for guidance in the spiritual life, will chiefly dwell. But those who are interested in her picture of the *via mystica* will turn rather to the exquisite chapters on prayer which develop the Similitude of the Waters.

Even when most objective, St. Teresa is always warm and human; and it is highly significant that the earliest of the figures of speech by which she is popularly remembered should be clearly traceable to her own experience. She loved water, and anything to do with it—wells, streams, rivers, sea, ships: everything. Even as a child she had knelt before a picture of Christ at the Samarian well and prayed: 'Lord, give me this water.'[25] And, though she could not often be at Alba de Tormes, where she had a view of the river from her very bed,[26] such views were continually in her mind's eye, and when she came to search for a similitude she had always one ready to hand:

> I cannot find anything more apt for the explanation of certain spiritual things than this element of water; for, as I am very ignorant and my wit gives me no help and I am so fond of this element, I have looked at it more attentively than at other things.[27]

From the image of water it was not far to travel to the picture of a watered garden; and, as the seclusion of a

[24] L. XL (I, 298).
[25] L. XXX (I, 203).
[26] LL, 51 (January 1574). Cf. also 326, 375; and pp. 156–7 below.
[27] I.C., IV, ii.

garden, or a cloister garth, must often have made her think of the life of contemplation, the different methods of watering a garden struck her as an apt representation of the contemplative's progress.

> The beginner must think of himself as of one setting out to make a garden in which the Lord is to take His delight, yet in soil most unfruitful and full of weeds. His Majesty uproots the weeds and will set good plants in their stead. Let us suppose that this is already done—that a soul has resolved to practise prayer and has already begun to do so. We have now, by God's help, like good gardeners, to make these plants grow, and to water them carefully, so that they may not perish, but may produce flowers which shall send forth great fragrance to give refreshment to this Lord of ours, so that He may often come into the garden to take His pleasure and have His delight among these virtues.[28]

How is a garden watered? There seemed to Teresa to be four ways. First, the water could be taken from a well—a laborious proceeding which later, no doubt, she often witnessed in her own convents. Secondly—a variant of this method—'by a water-wheel and buckets, when the water is drawn by a windlass': 'I have sometimes drawn it in this way,' she adds—no doubt in the garden at home: 'it is less laborious than the other and gives more water.' Thirdly, 'by a stream or a brook, which waters the ground much better, for it saturates it more thoroughly and there is less need to water it often.' Fourthly, 'by heavy rain, when the Lord waters it with no labour of ours, a way incomparably better than any of those which have been described.'[29]

To these four operations correspond four steps of prayer. Notice that St. Teresa takes for granted the weeding of the garden—the necessary discipline and self-purgation: even beginners in prayer attend to that. And it is they who draw the water by hand. Without vision, without mystical experience, without emotional exaltation, they toil at keeping their senses recollected, 'which is a great

[28] L. XI (I, 65).
[29] *Ibid.*

labour, because they have been accustomed to a life of distraction.'[30] They must learn 'to pay no heed to what they see or hear,' especially during prayer; to spend much time alone; to practise the often fatiguing exercise of meditation. For days the well will be dry and the beginner will suffer intolerable aridity: 'he would give it up entirely if he did not remember that he is pleasing and serving the Lord of the garden.'[31] But he will persevere, and resolve, 'even if this aridity should persist his whole life long, never to let Christ fall beneath the Cross.'[32]

The second degree of prayer—the water-wheel—represents that state of recollection called the Prayer of Quiet, of which Teresa first learned from Osuna. The understanding, which has laboured so hard in the first degree, is now at rest, and with it the memory; only the will is active, but it 'allows itself to be imprisoned by God, as one who well knows itself to be the captive of Him Whom it loves.'[33] In this state it must remain, even though the understanding and the memory return and attempt to distract it. For God is at work: He has planted in the soul a 'little spark' from His great fire, which it must neither quench when it comes nor endeavour to enkindle by its own efforts.[34]

In the third degree, in which the garden is watered by a river or spring, God 'may almost be said to be the gardener Himself, for it is He Who does everything.'[35] To this degree St. Teresa first attained only some five or six years before writing and for a long time she was quite unable to describe it. The faculties—understanding, memory and will—though not completely united with God, are all asleep to the world and can occupy themselves only with God. Therefore to the world this state is folly

[30] L. XI (I, 66).
[31] Ibid.
[32] L. XI (I, 67).
[33] L. XIV (I, 83).
[34] L. XV (I, 90–1).
[35] L. XVI (I, 96).

and madness—but it is 'a glorious folly, a heavenly madness, in which true wisdom is acquired, and a mode of fruition in which the soul finds its greatest delight.'[36]

Lastly comes the fourth degree—the highest which St. Teresa knew when she wrote her *Life*. Under the figure of rain—a lovelier and more precious image in barren Castile than in our humid north—she describes the union of all the faculties with God. She can do this only by searching for similitudes, first of one kind and then of another. 'It is described in mystical theology,' she explains apologetically, 'but I am unable to use the proper terms. . . . They all seem the same to me.'[37] What she can describe is the feelings of the soul in this state, for she herself knows them. It seems to be 'fainting almost completely away, in a kind of swoon, with an exceeding great and sweet delight.'[38] Bodily strength weakens; speech is impossible; nothing can be apprehended with the senses. The experience is a short one—'so at least it was with me'—not exceeding half-an-hour, though it may be some hours before the subject is normal again.[39] Not infrequently this fourth degree of prayer is accompanied by such supernatural phenomena as rapture, elevation and flight of the spirit.[40] But, in whatever form it is manifested, the essential point about it is the certain assurance which it brings of the very presence of God. 'The soul feels close to God and . . . there abides within it such a certainty that it cannot . . . do other than believe.'[41] At one time, St. Teresa thought this impossible; and yet:

> I could not cease believing that He was there, for it seemed almost certain that I had been conscious of His very presence. Unlearned persons would tell me that He was there only by grace; but I could not believe that, for, as I say, He seemed to me to be really

36 *Ibid.*
37 L. XVIII (I, 106).
38 L. XVIII (I, 108).
39 L. XVIII (I, 109–10).
40 L. XX (I, 119 ff.), *passim.*
41 L. XVIII (I, 110).

present; and so I continued to be greatly distressed. From this doubt I was freed by a very learned man of the Order of the glorious Saint Dominic:[42] he told me that He was indeed present and described how He communicated Himself to us, which brought me very great comfort.[43]

The foregoing summary, like any other that one may make of St. Teresa, has achieved little unless it sends the reader to the Saint herself. For one thing, it has robbed her descriptions of all their beauty—rich as they are with metaphors of fire and flame, light and darkness, cloud and water, flowers and fruit. It gives only a faint idea of the abundance of detail which she lavishes upon her sublime experiences. Nor can it convey anything of the simplicity, combined with a transparent sincerity, with which she wrote of these experiences, and which led so many to believe in her who might otherwise have thought her the victim of delusions. But, let it be repeated, the only way to get to know St. Teresa is to read her. This applies to her character and personality as well as to her doctrine, and to none of her works is it more applicable than to the *Life*.

A few words should be added here upon the *Spiritual Relations*, a group of narratives varying in length from two or three sentences to several pages, written by St. Teresa but collected by her editors. In the most recent Spanish edition of her works there are sixty-seven of them, but the first six are much more substantial than the rest and extend over the whole period covered by the series—from 1560 to 1581. Several of them are quoted in the pages which follow, but they are referred to at this point as a whole because they are essentially the appendix to a spiritual autobiography. This was evident to her first editor, the Salamancan professor Fray Luis de León; and the procedure which he adopted of printing such of the *Relations* as he possessed at the end of the *Life* has been followed in subsequent editions, though some of the shorter

42 Probably P. Báñez.
43 L. XVIII (I, 111).

narratives of which the dates are known have been inter-spersed among the *Letters*.

In the shorter *Relations* St. Teresa jots down the details of individual experiences—sometimes, it would seem, for the information of her confessors; sometimes, perhaps, for incorporation in one of her later books. From them her biographers have gleaned a number of characteristic anecdotes. One, for example, gives the well-known story of how St. John of the Cross, when acting as confessor to the nuns of the Incarnation, divided the Host between the Prioress and another sister—'because he wanted to mortify me, for I had told him that I was very pleased when the Hosts were large ones.'[44] Another describes her vision of Our Lady and the holy angels in the chapel of the Incarna-tion during the same period.[45] Several more describe her relations with the young friar Jerónimo Gracián.[46] Quite a number, on the other hand, are mere jottings—chips of the same precious metal which can be mined in such abundance from the *Life*:

On one occasion I learned how the Lord is in all things, and how He is in the soul, and the comparison suggested itself to me of a sponge absorbing water.[47]

Once, when I was wishing I could do something in Our Lord's service, I considered how little I could do to serve Him, and I said to myself: 'Why, Lord, dost Thou desire my works?' He answered: 'To see thy good will, daughter.'[48]

Once, when I was thinking how it distressed me to eat meat and do no penance, I heard these words: 'Sometimes there is more self-love in such a thought than desire for penance.'[49]

But it is the first six of the *Relations* that hold the series together. Like the *Life*, these were all written for the Saint's confessors and with the same purpose. They combine the

44 R. XXXV (I, 351).
45 R. XXV (I, 346). Cf. p. 109, below.
46 Notably R. XXXIX, XL (I, 354–6). Cf. p. 111, below.
47 R. XLV (I, 358).
48 R. LII (I, 361).
49 R. LXV (I, 366).

characteristics of the finest passages of the *Life*: simplicity, sincerity, vividness, picturesqueness, attention to detail. Indeed, it may be doubted if any of the accounts which she gives of her personal experiences surpass in lucidity the first of the *Relations*, written two years before the first draft of the *Life*, the third, which is approximately contemporaneous with it, or the fourth, written at Seville a year earlier than the *Interior Castle*. From this last may be quoted a characteristic and classical passage in which the Saint endeavours to answer a question put by her Jesuit confessor, P. Rodrigo Álvarez, about the nature of her intellectual visions:[50]

> She sees nothing, either inwardly or outwardly, for the vision is not imaginary. Yet, without seeing anything, the soul understands what it is, and it is pictured to her more clearly than if she were to see it, save that no exact picture is presented to her. It is as if a person were to feel that another is close beside her; and though, because of the darkness, he cannot be seen, she knows for certain that he is there. This, however, is not an exact comparison, for the person who is in the dark knows that the other is there, if not already aware of the fact, either by hearing a sound or by having seen him there previously. But in this case nothing of that kind happens: though not a word can be heard, either exteriorly or interiorly, the soul knows with perfect clearness who is there, where he is and sometimes what is meant by his presence. Whence he comes, and how, she cannot tell, but so it is, and for as long as it lasts she cannot cease to be aware of the fact. When the vision leaves her she cannot recall it to the imagination, however much she may wish to do so; for clearly, if she could, it would be a case of imagination and not of actual presence, to recapture which is not in her power.[51]

Though neither the longest nor the most widely known, the *Relation* which most appeals to Teresans will always be the sixth, written from Palencia, about eighteen months before her death, to her friend Don Alonso Velázquez, Bishop of Osma, whom she had first known when he was a Canon of Toledo, and whose gracious personality, as we

[50] Cf. p. 30, n. 9, above.
[51] R. IV (I, 326). Cf. L. XXVII (I, 171–2).

shall see, enters fleetingly but charmingly into the narrative of her last days.[52] The letters she wrote during this period are sad ones: her health had become worse; some of her dearest friends had died; the burdens of journeying and administration were growing too much for her. Yet inwardly she is as serene as ever. 'Any unrest and any strife can be borne,' she had written once, 'if we find *peace where we live*.'[53] 'Oh,' she begins, 'if only I could give Your Lordship a clear idea of the quiet and calm in which my soul now finds itself. For it is now so certain that it will have fruition of God that it seems to be in possession of it already.'[54]

'Peace where we live.' That was Teresa's dearest possession. And that is what makes the *Life*, with the *Relations*, so very much more than a conventional autobiography. From it we can draw strength, refreshment and inspiration. With its help we can replan our whole lives. Beneath its rippling surface we can discern the peace which passeth all understanding.

IV

THE *WAY OF PERFECTION*
(1565 ff.)

THE *Life* of St. Teresa is fundamental, not only to an understanding of its author's character and later career, but also in the rather curious sense that her other four major works are inseparably linked to it, each of them in quite a different way. The *Foundations* continues the story of her career precisely where the *Life* lays it down and carries it to a point only a few months from her death. The *Spiritual Relations* tells us more of her interior life down

---

[52] Cf. pp. 157, 159, below.
[53] I.C. IV (II, 235).
[54] R. VI (I, 334). A further account of this *Relation* will be found on p. 96, below.

to almost exactly the same place. The *Interior Castle* gives us an outline of the *via mystica* similar to that of Chapters XI to XXII of the *Life* but a very much longer and more detailed one: we can hardly doubt that it was these early chapters which, either to St. Teresa herself or to her advisers, suggested the writing of a more ambitious treatise. The *Way of Perfection* arises even more directly out of the *Life* than any of the others, and St. Teresa herself, in the preface to it, explains exactly how this happened.

The book was written, not at the command of the author's superiors or confessors, but at the earnest entreaty of the nuns of the first convent of the Reform. They must have known that the Mother Foundress had written an autobiography, though it is doubtful if any of them had read it, and they probably knew that, besides describing her own life, it contained a good deal of instruction about prayer. As it went into great detail concerning her most intimate spiritual experiences, it was unlikely (as she herself knew)[1] that they would be allowed access to it; so she obtained 'leaves'[2] from her confessor at the time, P. Báñez, to begin a new book, which should treat of 'certain things about prayer,' for the use of her daughters in religion.[3] This book would 'say something concerning the way and method of life which it is fitting should be practised in this house'[4] (i.e. at St. Joseph's, Ávila, and, as the author continues in her attractively inconsequent way, would also treat 'of other things, according as the Lord reveals them to me and as they come to my mind: since I do not know what I am going to say I cannot set it down in suitable order.'[5]

The book thus vaguely conceived was begun, as we gather from its preface, only 'a few days' after the com-

---

[1] W.P. Prologue (II, 2).
[2] W.P. Prologue (II, 1).
[3] *Ibid.*
[4] *Ibid.*
[5] W.P. Prologue (II, 2).

pletion of the *Life*[6]—that is, at the end of 1565 or early in the year following. When it was finished we cannot say, though it is noteworthy that on the last page St. Teresa holds out the hope that the nuns will be allowed to read the *Life* after all,[7] which may imply the lapse of some considerable time. On the other hand, she was in the mood for writing just then; and for something like eighteen months she had ample time for it. So, on balance, the probability would seem to be that the book was finished quickly.

Before saying more about it, we should refer to the most curious of its characteristics. It has come down to us in two manuscripts, each in an excellent state of preservation and each in St. Teresa's own hand. And these manuscripts are very different from each other. The earlier, preserved in the library of the Escorial, has 73 very short chapters; the later, in the possession of the Discalced Carmelite nuns of Valladolid, has 42 longer ones. The Escorial MS. undoubtedly represents the work as St. Teresa originally wrote it, for her twelve Avilan nuns and for no one else. Its style, even for her, is unusually natural—often quite colloquial; its language as affectionately intimate as though it were a bundle of letters. Its illustrations and figures of speech are unpretentious, generally homely, sometimes rather trivial. For some years—we cannot tell for how many—this was the only version of the *Way of Perfection* in existence. But when St. Teresa had made many other foundations, and could no longer keep in continual personal touch with all her daughters, she began to think that the book which she had written for them could do with revision. It was then that she sat down to rewrite the whole book, and this Valladolid redaction—no mere amended version but a new and free treatment of the theme with the original manuscript as a guide—is the result.

As she rewrote her book, she became increasingly con-

[6] W.P. Prologue (II, 2, n. 4).
[7] W.P. XLII (II, 186; cf. n. 6).

scious of its failings. She never had any illusions about her
gifts as an author: in her preface, as so often elsewhere, she
refers to 'the imperfection and the poverty of my style.'[8]
But until she began to reread it critically, she had evidently
not realized how bad the style of that first version was.
She must certainly compress some of those long rambling
sentences, omit redundant clauses, and aim at greater
clarity and precision of language. Then the chapters—
there were far too many of them. Originally, perhaps, a
chapter may merely have indicated the amount that she
wrote at a sitting, or the amount that she thought the
Avilan nuns capable of taking in at once. There was no
question, at the time, of others seeing her work: 'What
would happen,' she wrote, 'if these lines should be seen
outside this house? What would all the nuns say of me?'[9]
And now, it seemed, her homely pages were to become a
real book, and be copied out for her foundations all over
the country—perhaps, in time, to go to other countries. So
she must really reconsider its construction, arrange its
chapters according to theme, and give it symmetry and
unity. Some of the illustrations she had used, too, were not
quite proper: she had laughed about them with the nuns at
St. Joseph's: *they* knew well enough what she meant; but
others, unacquainted with her—and who knew, the book
might even be read for some time after her death!—would
be shocked, rather than edified, by them. There was that
metaphor, for example, about people who watched a bull-
fight from a grand-stand being safer than the men who
exposed themselves to a thrust from the bull's horns.[10] It
was effective, of course; it had quite thrilled the little circle
of nuns when she had first read it to them—but was it quite
the thing that a Discalced Carmelite ought to talk about?[11]

[8] W.P. Prologue (II, 1).
[9] W.P. XI (II, 48).
[10] W.P. XXXIX (II, 172).
[11] Luis de León, I am glad to say, evidently thought it was, and
included it in his edition of her works.

And, worse still, there was the chapter in which she had likened the contemplative life to a game of chess, in which the Divine King is checkmated by Humility. She had been a little doubtful about that even while she was writing it: in fact, she had appended a kind of playful apology:

> Now you will reprove me for talking about games, as we do not play them in this house and are forbidden to do so. That will show you what kind of a mother God has given you—she even knows about vanities like this![12]

But no playful apology would meet the case now. Attractive and apt as that similitude was, and carefully as she had phrased her interpretation of it lest she should be guilty of irreverence, it must be omitted from the book altogether.

It was on these lines that the Valladolid manuscript was built; and, as we compare it with the other, we cannot fail to see that it represents St. Teresa at her maturest and best. Her shrewdness, realism and complete lack of vanity make her a far abler reviser of her own work than might be expected of one who revised so little as she wrote. And yet the Escorial manuscript, with its wonderful freshness and spontaneity, is so faithful a reflection of its author's personality that none who love her can endure its being consigned to oblivion. So, as a rule, Spanish editors, while reproducing the later manuscript, have incorporated phrases and passages from the earlier, and the majority of English editors have followed their example. But the most recent and best Spanish editions have given both redactions in full and the excellent edition of the Benedictines of Stanbrook follows them so far as to embody passages translated from the Escorial manuscript in the Valladolid text. In my own translation, I have thought it preferable to interpolate only the outstanding passages omitted from E (Escorial) in what is essentially a translation of V (Valladolid), indicating them by italic type, and giving all

[12] W.P. XVI (II, 63).

other variants from E in footnotes. The reader can therefore see, almost at a glance, what St. Teresa intended to be read by her little family at St. Joseph's and also how she intended her work to appear in its definitive form.[13]

This brief note on the two manuscripts will, I hope, be forgiven me by any who find it without interest, since it is really necessary for the reader of the *Way of Perfection* who wants to know exactly what he has before him. And now we can look into it and find what it is all about. For a book which its author professed to be writing in so haphazard a fashion it is surprisingly well arranged. After a preamble comprising the preface and the first three chapters, it can be divided, with a fair degree of exactness, into three parts. The first of these (Chapters IV–XV) is mainly domestic, treating first of the principles which underlie adherence to the Rule of the Order—mutual love, detachment and humility—and going on to lay down precepts of perfection and to prescribe simple remedies suitable for communities suffering from minor disorders. The next section (Chapters XVI–XXVI), beginning with the similitude of the Game of Chess, leads us into themes more closely connected with the life of prayer. What is meant by the contemplative life; how some are unfitted for it; what impediments the contemplative may expect to meet; a comparison between mental and vocal prayer; and so on. During the latter part of this exposition St. Teresa makes frequent reference to the Lord's Prayer, and this may have given her the idea of devoting the remainder of her book (Chapters XXVII–XLII) to a commentary upon it. These chapters are deservedly the best known, both for their spirituality and for their arresting figures of speech. The commentary proceeds petition by petition, and has a good deal to say of the different stages of the contemplative life, particularly of the Prayer of Recollection and the Prayer

---

[13] Fuller details of the procedure I have adopted will be found in C.W. II, xxiii-xxv.

of Quiet. It ends with three chapters on the love and fear of God, 'two strong castles whence we can wage war on the world and on the devils,'[14] followed by a final chapter in which the author begs God to preserve her daughters from the world's perils. Then, most characteristically, she comes to an abrupt end:

> Well, sisters, Our Lord seems not to want me to write any more, for, although I had intended to go on, I can think of nothing to say.[15]

The first of the three sections will be of less interest to those who are reading St. Teresa for spiritual counsel (other, of course, than her own daughters) than to those who, attracted by her personality, are anxious to form as exact a picture as possible of her first family. And such will delight in these early chapters. The *Life* has told of the self-questionings that preceded Teresa's decision to found her first convent without an endowment. The *Way of Perfection* reflects, and answers, similar questionings in the minds of the nuns. They must not worry about food, or think they will get it by 'going about trying to please people.' Nor will worrying bring in money. They must not so much endure poverty as desire it.[16] Their houses must be 'small and poor in every way,' like the birthplace of Our Lord: 'any corner is sufficient for thirteen poor women.'

> As for a large ornate convent, with a lot of buildings—God preserve us from that! Always remember that these things will all fall down on the Day of Judgment, and who knows how soon that will be?
>
> It would hardly look well if the house of thirteen poor women made a great noise when it fell, for those who are really poor must make no noise....[17]

[14] W.P. XL (II, 173).
[15] W.P. XLII (II, 186). This passage is in E only, an indication which will be given in the following pages thus: (E). Interesting variants from E to the quotations in the text will often be found in C.W.
[16] W.P. II, *passim* (II, 5–9).
[17] W.P. II (II, 9).

Then, too, their little 'porch of Bethlehem' is not merely a home for them. It must be a 'little castle,' and they, with their own officers—'that is, the preachers and theologians'—must be its garrison: none of them must ever go over to the enemy.[18] How we seem to hear the Mother Foundress developing such simple and vivid metaphors for the benefit of faint-hearted sisters who had not realized what holy poverty would mean!

Next she guides their thoughts into constructive channels. They must cultivate mutual love. In some communities private friendships might be permissible, 'but in this house, where there are not, and can never be, more than thirteen nuns, all must be friends with each other, love each other; be fond of each other and help each other.'[19] The Discalced must never use such affectionate expressions as 'My darling!' or 'My love!': 'let such endearing words be kept for your Spouse, for you will be so often and so much alone with Him that you will want to make use of them all.'[20] A large part of their time was, in fact, spent in their cells, since 'getting used to solitude is a great help to prayer.'[21] For that reason St. Joseph's had no *casa de labor*, or common-room, where the nuns could work and talk together. But during their few recreation hours they must 'contrive' to enjoy themselves 'for the whole of the allotted time' even if they felt disinclined to do so, for that was part of perfect love.[22]

In this way, little by little, these chapters build up a picture of the community, with its open or latent virtues and its inevitable defects:[23] of the prioress giving 'heavy punishments' to nuns who 'make trouble'—imprisoning them in their cells, or sending them to other convents; of

[18] W.P. III (II, 10). Cf. pp. 78–9, below.
[19] W.P. IV (II, 17).
[20] W.P. VII (II, 35).
[21] W.P. IV (II, 18).
[22] W.P. VII (II, 34).
[23] W.P. VII, VIII, *passim* (II, 30–9).

the nuns trying to spare their sisters household work, being cross with each other 'because of some hasty word,' striving to subdue an excessive attachment to their relatives; and learning not to pamper their bodies—though 'in this house,' adds Teresa, tersely, 'there is very little chance for us to.'[24] Still, there are degrees of indulgence; and, in her early years at St. Joseph's, the Mother Foundress was disposed to be caustic about nuns who went sick on the slightest provocation.

> We do not keep the smallest points in the Rule, such as silence, which is quite incapable of harming us. Hardly have we begun to imagine that our heads are aching than we stay away from choir, though that would not kill us either. *One day we are absent because we had a headache some time ago; another day, because our head has just been aching again; and on the next three days in case it should ache once more....*
>
> But why, you will say, does the Prioress excuse us? Perhaps she would not if she knew what was going on inside us; but *she sees one of you wailing about a mere nothing as if your heart were breaking, and you come and ask her to excuse you from keeping the whole of your Rule ... and* there is always a physician at hand to confirm (what you say) or some friend or relative weeping at your side. *Sometimes the poor Prioress sees that your request is excessive, but* what can she do? She feels a scruple if she thinks she has been lacking in charity and she would rather the fault were yours than hers: *she thinks, too, that it would be unjust of her to judge you harshly.*[25]

When she rewrote the passage, however, Teresa omitted the trenchant phrases which I have italicized: perhaps, by that time, under her robust rule, the *malades imaginaires* were beginning to disappear.

Still, few of us, if we are honest, can profess any great superiority over the nuns of St. Joseph's, for even if the lines just quoted do not prick our conscience we shall hardly read on much farther unscathed. When the Mother Prioress chides her daughters for harbouring grievances because others are preferred to them, for attaching undue importance to their reputation, for excusing themselves

[24] W.P. X (II, 44).
[25] W.P. X (II, 45). The italicized clauses are found in E only. See also II, 45, n. 5.

when they are blamed, even if unjustly, for using 'such phrases as "I had right on my side," "They had no right to do this to me," "The person who treated me like this was not right," '[26] we begin to realize how high was the standard set by the Mother who in setting it did not hesitate to say of herself: 'I must confess I have made very little progress.'[27] The very fact that she could be bold enough to draw aside the veil which hid the community at St. Joseph's from the censorious world bears witness to the earnestness of the lives that were lived there. St. Teresa could never have said of the Incarnation, as she said of St. Joseph's: 'This house is another Heaven, if it be possible to have Heaven upon earth.'[28]

In the second section, before coming to her Divine Chessgame, St. Teresa writes at length about the placing of the pieces—for 'you may be sure that anyone who cannot set out the pieces in a game of chess will never be able to play well, and, if he does not know how to give check, he will not be able to bring about a checkmate.'[29] First, she reminds her daughters, 'it does not follow that, because all of us in this house practise prayer, we are all perforce to be contemplatives.'[30] What we must all be is humble: contemplation is 'something given by God, and, as it is not necessary for salvation and God does not ask it of us before He gives us our reward, we must not suppose that anyone else will require it of us.'[31] There is as much room for different types in a religious community as there is in the world—or in Heaven. Martha 'was holy, but we are not told she was a contemplative.'

Remember that there must be someone to cook the meals, and count yourselves happy in being able to serve like Martha.[32]

[26] W.P. XIII (II, 54).
[27] W.P. XV (II, 59).
[28] W.P. XIII (II, 57).
[29] W.P. XVI (E) (II, 63).
[30] W.P. XVII (II, 69).
[31] *Ibid.*
[32] W.P. XVII (II, 70-1).

That last sentence, with its flash of sanctified common-sense, is the kind of aphorism one continually lights upon in this most practical of treatises, which is one reason why, to many who in the *Interior Castle* find little, as it were, to take hold of, it is so precious. All the pages in which the author reasons with those who are fretting because they can barely meditate, 'offer'—to quote a chapter-heading —'great consolation to actives.'[33] Let them do what they can, as well as they can, and God will reward them. There is a striking passage here which aims at consoling actives, but also warns contemplatives that they will have no shel-tered life, but as hard a time as any. Note in it once more a flash of the Saint's intensely human and endearing personality—the words italicized in the text, which un-fortunately she omitted in her definitive version:

> Go cheerfully about whatever services you are ordered to do, as I have said: if such a servant is truly humble she will be blessed in her active life, and will never make any complaint save of herself. *I would much rather be like her than like some contemplatives.* Leave others to wage their own conflicts, which are not light ones. The standard-bearer is not a combatant, yet none the less he is exposed to great danger, and, inwardly, must suffer more than anyone, for he cannot defend himself, as he is carrying the standard, which he must not allow to leave his hands, even if he is cut to pieces. Just so contemplatives have to bear aloft the standard of humility and must suffer all the blows which are aimed at them without striking any themselves. Their duty is to suffer as Christ did, to raise the Cross on high and not to allow it to leave their hands, whatever the perils in which they find themselves.[34]

The same kind of hortatory consolation is given to those who find difficulty in meditation. Restless by temperament, they are like unbroken horses—'no one can stop them: now they go this way, now that way; they are never still.'[35] Or (and here Teresa's pen quickens its speed and her eyes sparkle as her favourite image comes into her mind) they

[33] W.P. XVIII (II, 72).
[34] W.P. XVIII (II, 73–4).
[35] W.P. XIX (II, 77).

are like 'people who are very thirsty and see water a long way off, yet, when they try to go to it, find someone who all the time is barring their path.'[36] Then comes a characteristic disquisition on the properties of water, which lengthens the chapter out of all proportion, but leads up to the following simple but beautiful conclusion:

> Remember, the Lord invites us all; and, since He is truth itself, we cannot doubt Him. If His invitation were not a general one, He would not have said: 'I will give you to drink.' He might have said: 'Come, all of you, for after all you will lose nothing by coming; and I will give drink to those whom I think fit for it.' But, as He said we were all to come, without making this condition, I feel sure that none will fail to receive this living water unless they cannot keep to the path.[37]

Another of Teresa's preliminary themes is determination. Here, as so often in this book, she is virile to the last degree. For those who would lead the life of prayer, it is 'most important—all-important, indeed'—that they should resolve never to turn back, 'whatever may come, whatever may happen to them, however hard they may have to labour, whoever may complain of them ... whether the very world dissolves before them.'[38] They will meet all kinds of objections:

> Again and again people will say to us: 'It is dangerous,' 'So-and-so was lost through doing this,' 'Someone else got into wrong ways,' 'Some other person, who was always praying, fell just the same' ..., 'It is not meant for women ...,' 'They would do better to stick to their spinning,' 'These subtleties are of no use to them.'[39]

Exactly the same arguments, in almost exactly the same words, are used to-day. Strange how little the language of the world has varied in four centuries!

And Teresa is not slow in meeting the world with its

36 *Ibid.*
37 W.P. XIX (II, 85).
38 W.P. XXI (II, 89).
39 *Ibid.*

own arguments. 'Worldly people like to take life peaceably; but they will deny themselves sleep, perhaps for nights on end, in order to gain a farthing's profit, and they will leave other people no peace either of body or of soul.'[40] And how much greater are their risks than ours! 'Sooner or later, they will die of thirst.'[41]

These and similar admonitions having 'prepared the board,' Teresa goes on to explain the meaning of mental prayer—a term of which 'a great many people ... seem terrified.'[42] She takes it first in its simplest sense, as equivalent to a mere thinking of what we are saying when we recite our prayers. For pages on end, with a patience amazing in one who had herself reached such heights, she expounds quite elementary principles, as a mother might to little children. Only with people who 'tell you that you are speaking to God by reciting the Paternoster and thinking of worldly things'[43] is she unable to reason at all. With this form of 'mental prayer' she contrasts perfect contemplation,' in which 'it is His Majesty Who does everything; the work is His alone and far transcends human nature.'[44] That may come to us, or it may not; we must not worry about it. Let us simply learn to say our prayers better.

So—again as if she were talking to a child—she takes an imaginary daughter by the hand, and explains to her, simply and affectionately, what she must do when she kneels down to say her prayers:

> As you are alone, you must look for a companion.... Imagine that this Lord Himself is at your side.... Believe me, you should stay with so good a Friend for as long as you can before you leave Him.... Do you think it is a small thing to have such a Friend as that beside you?[45]

[40] W.P. XXI (II, 90).
[41] W.P. XXI (II, 91).
[42] W.P. XXIV (II, 101).
[43] W.P. XXII (II, 93).
[44] W.P. XXV (II, 105). The state described would be either the Third or the Fourth Water (pp. 56–7, above).
[45] W.P. XXVI (II, 106).

That first. And don't be frightened, she continues. 'I am not asking you now to think of Him, or to form numerous conceptions of Him, or to make long and subtle meditations with your understanding. I am asking you only to look at Him.'[46] As she recalls the lessons she had learned so long before from the Fathers of the Society she becomes appealing, even eloquent. 'You are capable of looking at very ugly and loathsome things: can you not, then, look at the most beautiful thing imaginable?' Though, of course —with a flash almost of playfulness—'if you do not think Him so, I give you leave to stop.'[47]

> (But) your Spouse never takes His eyes off you, daughters.... Is it such a great matter, then, for you to avert the eyes of your soul from outward things and sometimes to look at Him? See, He is only waiting for us to look at Him.... If you want Him you will find Him. He longs so much for us to look at Him once more that it will not be for lack of effort on His part if we fail to do so.[48]

This must suffice for a glimpse of Teresa the teacher. She now goes on to counsel her daughters on means and aids to recollection, none of which are surer than those of the Lord Himself. In this way her talk on mental prayer shades effortlessly into an exposition of the Lord's Prayer.

The third section may be regarded from two standpoints. In the first place, it is an exquisite commentary on the sublimest and most comprehensive of all short prayers, so simple that the most unlearned can read it and profit by it for themselves: I shall not attempt to paint the lily by discoursing upon it. But with her exposition St. Teresa tries to combine a commentary on the *via mystica*; 'for ... in the Paternoster the Lord has taught us the whole method of prayer and of high contemplation, from the very beginnings of mental prayer to Quiet and Union.'[49] She confines

[46] W.P. XXVI (II, 107).
[47] W.P. XXVI (II, 107). The last sentence is found in E only.
[48] W.P. XXVI (II, 107).
[49] W.P. XXXVII (II, 161).

herself to the intermediate stages, for of the lowest she had written earlier in the book, and of the highest she had less experience than twelve years later, when she sat down to write those exquisite final chapters of the *Interior Castle*. It was of the Prayer of Quiet and the Prayer of Union—corresponding approximately to the second and third of the Waters—that she was anxious to write here; and also of the Prayer of Recollection, a state leading into the Prayer of Quiet, which she had not fully distinguished from it when she wrote her *Life*, though in the *Interior Castle*, as we shall see, she treats it in some detail.

Her particular purpose here seems to have been to present ideas which would be quite new, and perhaps rather frightening, to many of her daughters, in a context with which they would all be familiar. That is good psychology. 'I am speaking only about the way to recite vocal prayers well,' she says. 'I am discussing vocal prayer here.' 'I attach great importance to your saying your vocal prayers well.'[50] She wants to do away with the hard-and-fast distinction usually made between vocal prayer and mental, by showing that the two are interrelated, that the latter must give life to the former and that it is possible to pass from the former to the latter more quickly and readily than is generally believed. The ease with which she approaches the subject of the Prayer of Quiet is masterly. 'If it were not that you would tell me I am treating of contemplation'—that 'terrifying' word again!—'it would be appropriate . . . to say a little about the beginning of pure contemplation, which those who experience it call the Prayer of Quiet.'[51] And, before doing so, she tells her daughters that 'there are many people who practise vocal prayer in the manner already described and are raised by God to the higher kind of contemplation without knowing

[50] W.P. XXIX, XXX (II, 121, 125). Some of these phrases, however, occur in E only, so the Saint may have thought later that she had been over-emphatic here.
[51] W.P. XXX (II, 125).

how it has happened.'[52] Then comes the description of Quiet, which corresponds very closely to that given in the *Life*, but is reinforced by two simple and beautiful images —the harmony between husband and wife, and the infant at its mother's breast: 'such is the mother's care for it that she gives it its milk without its having to ask for it so much as by moving its lips. That is what happens here.'[53]

Looking at these chapters as they stand, one might fear that, without further guidance, readers would too readily suppose themselves to have attained these supernatural states. There is a difference, for example, between the habit of recollection and the Prayer of Recollection which is not very clearly brought out in a sentence from Chapter XXVIII: 'If one prays in this way, the prayer may be only vocal, but the mind will be recollected much sooner; and this is a prayer which brings with it many blessings.'[54] Or again: 'If we cultivate the habit, make the necessary effort and practise the exercises for several days, the benefits will reveal themselves, and when we begin to pray we shall realize that the bees are coming to the hive and entering it to make the honey, and all without any effort of ours.'[55] Though, as St. Teresa very truly avers, God gives His gifts to whom He wills and as He wills, irrespectively of rule, there can be few who attain to the Prayer of Recollection, in the sense in which the term is used in the *Interior Castle*, after only 'several days,' and yet there may be many who are misled into thinking that they have received it thus quickly. Though modern readers of the *Way of Perfection* need to be reminded of this, however, we must remember that its first readers were living under direction and would therefore be less likely to go astray. In the Escorial manuscript there is a significant warning, which, when she rewrote the book, St. Teresa thought it

52 *Ibid.*
53 W.P. XXXI (II, 131).
54 W.P. XXVIII (II, 115).
55 W.P. XXVIII (II, 116).

practicable to omit—probably because her nuns were better instructed by that time than earlier.[56] Present-day readers, nevertheless, may do well to bear it in mind:

> Anyone who has had experience of this kind of prayer will understand quite well what I am saying if, after reading this, she considers it carefully, and thinks out its meaning: otherwise it will be Greek (*algarabía*) to her.[57]

But inability to understand a small part of this book will not obscure its charm or rob it of its inspiration. It contains the Saint's most practical pages—which is saying a good deal, for the more one reads her, the more keenly one feels that her mission in life was less to found Carmelite convents than to help millions everywhere to live the life of prayer. There is not a chapter in the book which fails to give the receptive reader the impression that he is being taken in hand by the surest-footed of guides familiar with every inch of the road.

It is also the most vigorous of her books, written when she was at the very height of her powers. Though yielding nothing, either in picturesqueness, or in love's eloquence, to the *Life* or the *Interior Castle*, the *Way of Perfection* has a terseness and a directness of attack which she equals nowhere else. It never rambles, or dissolves momentarily into formlessness, as some of the other books tend to do. Teresa rightly disclaims artistic effect: 'You may understand (this) better as expressed in my rough style than in other books which put it more elegantly.'[58] But that 'rough style' has brought her into the first rank of Spanish prose-writers and those who consider the *Way of Perfection* her finest work are in the main those who think of her as a great writer rather than as a mystic or a saint. Take a few typical sentences:

[56] By 1573 (F. IV: III, 18) she could say that all but one or two nuns in each house had attained 'to perfect contemplation, and some of them ... to raptures.'
[57] W.P. XXXI (E) (II, 131).
[58] W.P. XVI (II, 68).

Those who really love God love all good, seek all good, help forward all good, praise all good, and invariably join forces with good men and help and defend them. They love only truth and things worthy of love. Do you think it possible that anyone who really and truly loves God can love vanities, riches, worldly pleasures or honours? Can he engage in strife or feel envy? No; for his only desire is to please the Beloved. . . .

There are degrees of love for God, which shows itself in proportion to its strength. If there is little of it, it shows itself but little; if there is much, it shows itself a great deal. But it always shows itself, whether little or much, provided it is real love for God.[59]

What could be simpler, clearer, more vigorous, more penetrating than that?

And the style of the book is the mirror of its thought and teaching. One of the best known of the phrases ascribed to St. Teresa is 'Be as strong men.' It would be better known still were it quoted in its correct form and in its context. It occurs in a passage where the Saint is exhorting her daughters not to use extravagant expressions of friendship. 'There is no reason for you to use them,' she says (and note once more the vigour and terseness of the language):

They are very effeminate; and I should not like you to be that, or even to appear to be that, in any way, my daughters; I want you to *be strong men.* If you do all that is in you, *the Lord will make you so manly that men themselves will be amazed at you.*[60]

It is by no chance that the *Way of Perfection* abounds in metaphors of warfare, opening with a declaration of war upon the Lutherans and containing the most familiar of its author's martial allegories. Mother of the Counter-Reformation as well as of Carmel, Teresa began her Reform, so she tells us, in order to make such reply as she could to the 'harm and havoc that were being wrought in France by these Lutherans': 'my whole yearning was, and still is, that, as (the Lord) has so many enemies and so few

[59] W.P. XL (II, 173–4).
[60] W.P. VII (II, 35). Italics mine. Cf. p. 186, below.

friends, these last should be trusty ones.'[61] The situation
seemed to her 'like a war in which the enemy has overrun
the whole country, and the Lord of the country, hard
pressed, retires into a city, which he causes to be well fortified, whence from time to time he is able to attack.' Inside
the city is a garrison of 'picked men,' who 'can do more by
themselves than . . . (could) many soldiers if they were
cowards.'[62] The allegory continues at length and is pressed
home in detail, but the essence of it is that those 'picked
men'—those 'strong men'—are Teresa's own daughters.
Her order for the day is one of daring and defiance:

> We cannot be forced to surrender by hunger: we can die, but we
> cannot be conquered.[63]

Yes, Teresa had set her face like a flint; and it is for its
flint-like qualities that the *Way of Perfection* will always
be known.

V

FROM MEDINA TO PASTRANA
(1567–1569)

PERHAPS the full flavour of life in that first convent of the
Reform can be best extracted from a combination of the
hortatory passages of the *Way of Perfection* with the early
pages of the *Foundations*. This latter account of the activities of St. Teresa after 1567 was begun in 1573, when
memories of those precious years at St. Joseph's would still
have been fresh, and in its first chapters we can catch more
than a glimpse of the eager but immature little community
of thirteen progressing steadily towards sanctity. Some of
the nuns had come to the convent, after years in the
Incarnation, for the same reason as its foundress. Others,

[61] W.P. I (II, 3).
[62] W.P. III (II, 10). Cf. p. 68, above.
[63] W.P. III (II, 10).

however, 'the world seemed already to have claimed for its own, to judge by their showiness and curiosity';[1] and these had to be practised in virtues as fundamental as strict obedience, sometimes by methods which were extremely crude.[2] But, disciplined or not, those early nuns were tremendously in earnest. They delighted in poverty and solitude. Their 'only care was to serve and praise our Lord.' They obeyed the Apostolic injunction to rejoice always, and when they 'lacked anything, which was very seldom, they would rejoice all the more.'[3] Their saintly prioress was a true mother to them: 'they concealed none of their faults from me, however interior' and the favours, the lofty desires and the detachment which the Lord granted them were very great.'[4] One can well believe that, now she had found a way of life which seemed so well worth living, St. Teresa would have been content to devote herself to the training of such malleable young souls until God should take her home.

But this was not the state of life to which it had pleased Him to call her. At the mature age of fifty-two, with 'heroic intrepidity and apostolic zeal,' this valiant and vigorous woman was to enter upon a completely new life and to 'develop natural gifts which had hitherto lain dormant within her.'[5] She was to make, not one foundation for women, but seventeen. She was to be the moving spirit in the extension of the Reform to men. She was to 'face disapproval, unpopularity, jealousy, ridicule, disdain,' and 'to cope with physical trials which it is difficult for us now even to picture.'[6] She was to become the most prominent figure in the whole of her Order's history—the Mother of a reborn Carmel. And through her writings, so profound, so understanding and so tender, she was to influence

[1] F. I (III, 1).
[2] F. I (III, 2).
[3] F. I (III, 1).
[4] F. I (III, 3).
[5] P. Silverio de Santa Teresa. In C.W., III, xi.
[6] P. Silverio de Santa Teresa. In C.W., III, xi–xii.

Christian people, in all succeeding ages, everywhere.

It must have been in the late summer or early autumn of 1566 that St. Teresa received a visit at St. Joseph's, Ávila, from a Franciscan friar named Antonio Maldonado. He was a missionary, just back from the Indies, and he spoke with feeling to the little group of nuns about the millions of souls perishing there for lack of Christian teachers. Teresa, though one of her brothers was in the Indies, had perhaps never before had their awful plight so vividly put before her. There are many indications in her books of her distress at the heresies which were in ˙ading Europe, but at that time her vision extended only a ̇ ˙tle way beyond the Avilan walls. Before that missionary friar went on his way he had kindled a new flame. Not that, either then or at any other time, Teresa thought of going to the Indies herself. But she felt stirrings within her to do something more for her fellow Christians than she had done already; and one night, when she was debating this with herself, in 'terrible distress,' the Lord appeared to her 'in His usual way,' and said to her, 'very lovingly': 'Wait a little, daughter, and thou shalt see great things.'[7] The words remained so firmly fixed in her mind that she was unable to banish them. What they meant she could neither infer nor imagine, but they seemed proof to her that she was to be used in some new way.

In the early days of the next year it came to Teresa's ears that the General of her Order was to pay a visit to Spain. For a very good reason the news caused her disquiet. Such a visit was the rarest of occurrences and it was very natural that she should connect it with her attempts at reform. There was always the risk that her tiny foundation might be dissolved, or that she herself, at the least, might be sent back to the Incarnation and the Mitigated Rule. For the original attitude of her Provincial, it will be remembered, had led to the irregularity of making the new

[7] F. I (III, 4).

foundation subject to the Ordinary, instead of to the Order, and the General could hardly be expected to countenance that.

However, when on April 11, 1567, P. Rossi (or, to hispanize his name, as is usually done, P. Rubeo) arrived at Ávila, Teresa very soon discovered that her fears were groundless. She did not know (how could she?) that it was on a reforming mission that he had come to Spain, with the sanction of a Pope bent on reform, but she had decided, from her own insignificant end, to handle the situation firmly. So she sent him a personal invitation to visit St. Joseph's, where 'the Bishop was pleased that he should be shown all the respect which was paid to his own person.'[8] Having got him there, she spoke to him with that blend of charm, frankness and determination which had solved so many of her problems and was to solve many more.

> I told him my story quite truthfully and simply, for, whatever the consequences, I am always inclined to deal in that way with prelates, as they are in the place of God.[9]

To her delight and surprise, his judgment was altogether favourable. Not only did he assure her that he had no desire for her to leave, but he expressed his pleasure at seeing in the new convent 'a picture, however imperfect, of our Order as it had been in its early days' and the observance of 'the Primitive Rule in all its strictness.'[10] Indeed, he was anxious for further experiments of the same kind, so he gave Teresa patents for the foundation of more convents, in such a form as to override the possible objections of any future Provincial. Here, she thought, were already the beginnings of the 'great things' which had been promised her: and this belief was confirmed in the following August, when, at the joint request of herself and Don Álvaro de Mendoza, Bishop of Ávila, the General sent

[8] F. II (III, 5).
[9] Ibid.
[10] Ibid.

her authorizations for the foundation of two Reformed houses for men.[11]

But, before these documents arrived, Teresa had founded her second house for women. Her initial success with the General, like her earlier success with the foundation of St. Joseph's, had produced an emotional reaction; and, after P. Rubeo's departure, she found herself a prey to misgivings. It was all very well for him to give her permission to make these foundations, but where was she to find the means? She knew of no friars who were likely to embrace her Reform, and neither for monasteries nor for convents had she either houses or money. 'Here was a poor Discalced nun, without help from anywhere, except from the Lord, loaded down with patents and good wishes but devoid of all possibility of making them effective.'[12] But this mood, as before, soon passed:

> I was not devoid either of courage or of hope: as the Lord had given me the one, He would give the other. Everything seemed to me quite possible now and so I set to work.[13]

For her second convent she thought of Medina del Campo, a busy market-town, some fifty miles north-west of Ávila, with the distinction of possessing a royal residence. As her best friends, the Jesuits, had already a house there, she hoped they might help her in this, especially since its Rector, who was now also Provincial of the Society, was P. Baltasar Álvarez, her former confessor and friend.

This second convent, like the first, was to be founded without endowments; and the opposition which the proposal aroused was of much the same type as before, though the support for it was so much greater that it proved less severe. At Ávila, too, her friends shook their heads at her, while people in general said roundly that she was mad. Even the Bishop thought this project of going

[11] F. II (III, 7).
[12] F. II (III, 7).
[13] *Ibid.*

farther afield 'the height of folly,' though he was wise enough not to say so.[14]

The 'folly,' no doubt, lay in entertaining the project while completely without material resources. Though she had a licence, she had 'neither a house nor a farthing to buy one.'[15] However, the Lord was to provide. A girl who, for lack of accommodation, had had to be refused entry to St. Joseph's, heard that a new house was to be founded and asked to be admitted to it. As she had enough money, not indeed for buying a house, but for renting one, it was agreed that this should be the solution of the problem; and so, with two nuns from St. Joseph's and four from the Incarnation (including the Sub-Prioress), St. Teresa set out on the first of her many peregrinations. With her, too, went the chaplain of St. Joseph's, P. Julián de Ávila—a simple, trusting, devoted soul, one of the most attractive of her friends, who throughout her years of journeyings was to accompany her almost everywhere and to leave behind a collection of reminiscences which are among her biographer's principal sources.

Another prominent figure in the lives of the two great Carmelite Saints now comes into view—the Prior of the Carmelite monastery at Medina, Fray Antonio de Heredia, afterwards Antonio de Jesús. To this friar St. Teresa had written, asking him to find her a house in advance of her arrival, and, having succeeded in doing so, he came halfway to meet them. To Medina from Ávila was a two-day journey and they covered the longer and more trying part of it on the first day, spending the night in an inn at Arévalo, where Fray Antonio arrived on the next morning to escort them the rest of the way. When they reached Medina it was midnight, and the following day was the Feast of the Assumption (August 15).[16]

This was, of course, as it is still, one of the great holidays

14 F. III (III, 9).
15 F. III (III, 8).
16 F. III (III, 11).

of the Spanish year. Coming in the middle of the bull-fighting season, too, it is the one day when every town of any size, all over Spain, has its bull-fight. 'It was a great mercy on the part of the Lord,' wrote St. Teresa, 'that we met none of the bulls which were to fight on the next day and which at that time were being shut in.' Equally anxious not to meet human beings, they alighted at the monastery, 'in order not to make a noise,' and went to the house on foot.[17]

Thus far she had been quite satisfied with events; but when at the end of a long day's journey she set eyes on the house which Fray Antonio had found them she was aghast at it. 'The Lord must have been pleased that that blessed Father should have become blind or he would have seen that it was not fitting to put the Most Holy Sacrament in such a place.' Though small, it had seemed to his rather unpractical mind quite adequate, provided a chapel could be improvised in the porch by enclosing it with hangings. But, at the first glance, her woman's eyes saw that to make it even passable would mean their working all night. The walls were unplastered and in 'a very tumbledown condition' and the roof had holes in. All they could do was to clean and hang the porch so that Mass might be said in the morning. But unfortunately the owner, who had provided them with tapestry and damask, had not thought of nails. So they had to go round the house pulling nails out of the walls; and we can imagine the strange scene on that hot August night—some of the nuns on their knees scrubbing the floor of the porch, and others hanging the tapestry, with Father Julián hammering in the nails for them. By daybreak they had the makeshift chapel ready, the altar installed and the bell ringing; and, after Mass, which they witnessed 'through the chinks of the door, which was opposite the altar,' they saw the installation of the Most Holy Sacrament.[18]

[17] F. III (III, 11).
[18] F. III (III, 12).

But alas! they also saw a good deal more. Not only did the house look much worse by day than it had looked at midnight but parts of the walls had fallen down—no doubt some of the nails so ruthlessly extracted had been holding them together. It was the last straw. The two-day journey, followed by the busy sleepless night, produced the inevitable result upon Teresa's volatile temperament, and she found herself plunged into despair. A few days before, everything had seemed so easy; now, all at once, it had become impossible.

> I could think only of my weakness and lack of power. What good result could I hope for when I was relying on anything so miserable as myself? If I had been alone, I believe I could have endured it better; but to think that my companions would have to return to their houses, after all the opposition they had encountered before leaving, was a terrible trial to me.[19]

By evening, when Álvarez sent one of his fathers to see how the nuns were getting on, St. Teresa had decided that they would have to place a guard over the Sacrament and look for another house where they could live until their own was repaired. It took a week to find even part of one, during which time they lived in their tumbledown structure as well as they could, Teresa keeping vigil over the Sacrament by night through one of the windows: 'when the moon was very bright, I could see it easily.'[20] Eventually a Medina business man lent them the upper part of his own house, so that they were able to observe complete enclosure. The repair of the original house took fully two months and Teresa would not leave until it was finished.

It was while she was there, probably during the month of September, that she took the first important step towards making a foundation of the Reform for men.[21] Though Fray Antonio had not distinguished himself in the

[19] F. III (III, 12).
[20] F. III (III, 13).
[21] For another account of this part of her life, written from a slightly different standpoint, see *Spirit of Flame*, 9th impression, 1961, pp. 20 ff.

choice of the Medina house, she felt it wise, in view of his position, to begin by consulting him. To her surprise, she had no sooner told him of her wish to enlist some friars in the Reform than he offered himself as the first. She could not believe her ears:

> I took it for a joke and told him so; for although he was a good friar, given to recollection, very studious and fond of his cell, besides being a learned man, he did not seem to me to be at all the man for the beginning of such an enterprise: he had not sufficient spirituality, nor could he have endured the necessary privations, being delicate in health and not accustomed to them.[22]

He insisted that 'for many days' he had experienced the desire for a stricter life and had even thought of joining the Carthusians. But Teresa was 'not quite satisfied' and suggested his thinking it over for a year, during which time he could practise the Primitive Rule privately. 'Shortly afterwards,' she met the young friar from Salamanca University who was afterwards to be known as St. John of the Cross, and who also offered himself as a recruit, 'provided there were no long delay.' About this candidate she had no doubt whatsoever and waited to take the next step only till she should have 'a place to begin in.' Meanwhile Antonio went back to his monastery and his year's probation, while John returned to the University to take a final course in theology.[23]

By the November of 1567 the Medina house was running smoothly and 'the sisters there were walking in the very steps of those of St. Joseph's in Ávila.'[24] So Teresa went for a fortnight to visit her friend Doña Leonor de Mascareñas in Madrid, and then on to Alcalá de Henares, twenty miles in the other direction, for a consultation with the distinguished Dominican, P. Domingo Báñez, who had stood up for her, years before, at the famous joint meeting in Ávila, and whom she had last met, by pure chance, at

22 F. III (III, 14).
23 F. III (III, 15).
24 F. IX (III, 44).

Arévalo, on her way to the foundation at Medina.[25] No doubt, since he was so sympathetic, she discussed with him the whole of her plans for future foundations; at any rate, there was plenty of time for her to do so, as she stayed at Alcalá until the following February. Then she went southward to Toledo to see Doña Luisa de la Cerda, who persuaded her to make a third foundation at a strange little fortress-like town called Malagón, a few miles north of Ciudad Real. The town, or the greater part of it, being Doña Luisa's own property, she was naturally anxious to have one of her friend's convents there.

Notwithstanding her anxiety to please a wealthy and generous patroness, Teresa was doubtful about going to so small a place, for by this time she was completely wedded to the principle of doing without endowments and she could certainly not rely for support upon the people of Malagón. But Doña Luisa said she would provide them with enough money to live on, and, after consulting the usual 'learned men,' Teresa agreed. This time she did the journey in grand style, Doña Luisa herself accompanying her and the nuns for whom she had sent to make the foundation, and putting them all up for a week at her castle there, until, by Palm Sunday (April 11), 1568, their house was ready.[26]

This time, with the great lady behind them, there was no talk of opposition and no need for secrecy. No clandestine Mass, behind curtains, in the half-light of dawn, but a procession from the village winding its way up the hill to the castle and then returning to the Parish Church with the veiled sisters in their white mantles.[27] At the church a sermon was preached—and in a country with so impressive a standard of ecclesiastical oratory a sermon is always something of an event—and a fresh procession was then formed to take the Blessed Sacrament to the newly founded

25 F. III (III, 10).
26 F. IX (III, 46).
27 *Ibid.*

convent. For over a month she stayed there—there was 'so much to do'[28]—and not until the middle of May did she set out northwards to make a fourth foundation—at Valladolid.

This was a long journey, of some two hundred miles—perhaps the longest Teresa had made in her whole life. Twice she broke the first part of it—at Toledo, where she stayed in Doña Luisa's house during its owner's absence in Andalusia, and at Escalona, thirty miles farther north.[29] But the fifty hard, rough miles over the *sierras* between Escalona and Ávila must have been trying beyond endurance. She reached Ávila, 'extremely tired,' after travelling 'very slowly,' and it must have been a real rest to her to spend practically the whole of the month of June at her original St. Joseph's.

While there she received the offer of a little house in a neighbouring hamlet called Duruelo which would serve for her first monastery.[30] It was a mere cottage, in poor condition, but it was better than nothing[31] and it enabled her to make a beginning with this fresh venture. So in July, on her way northwards again, she called there and inspected it, before going on to Medina del Campo, where she found that both her friars were eager to start their new life: Fray Antonio, good soul, said that, if there were nothing better, he would start in a pig-sty.[32] She decided to take Fray John, the younger, brighter and more teachable of the two, to the Valladolid foundation, to gain all the experience he could of her methods. Meanwhile Fray Antonio was to busy himself in collecting necessaries for the Duruelo house, and, that done, to join Teresa at Valladolid and make final preparations.

The new house at Valladolid, given to St. Teresa several

[28] LL. 5 (May 18, 1568).
[29] LL. 6 (May 27, 1568).
[30] F. XIII (III, 62).
[31] Cf. *Spirit of Flame*, p. 22.
[32] F. XIII (III, 63).

months before by 'a young man, a person of some importance,' was the best they had yet had. Adjoining it were a
'fine big garden' and a 'large vineyard.'[33] On the other
hand, it was inconveniently far from the city and its nearness to the river made it unhealthily damp. They went in
on the Feast of the Assumption, 1568, but before long they
all began to suffer from the humidity and found it impossible to remain there. Fortunately they had a good friend
in the Bishop of Ávila's sister, Doña María de Mendoza,
who took the house off their hands and bought them
another. This they entered on February 3, 1569, with
'a fine procession which aroused great devotion in the
people.'[34] The period of unavoidable secrecy was now
definitely past and the principle of the Reform was
accepted by all.

The false start at Valladolid kept St. Teresa there until
the end of February but during that time Fray Antonio
and Fray John had got to work at Duruelo. On the last
day of September John left Valladolid, and two months
later he was joined by Antonio and a lay companion who
was to make the third of this tiny community.[35] On
Advent Sunday, November 28, 1568, John of the Cross,
Antonio of Jesus and Joseph of Christ took their new
vows, the first of a great company of Discalced friars who,
even in the first few decades of their history, included
many of unusual sanctity.

St. Teresa was able to write a good deal about their early
life, for, on leaving Valladolid for Toledo, she went
through Medina, Ávila and Madrid, and took in Duruelo,
which was on the direct road to Ávila, as well.[36] It was on
this occasion that an encounter took place which I have
already described in Teresa's own vivid words but which
will bear re-telling. As she approached the cottage, un-

[33] F. X (III, 46).
[34] F. X (III, 49).
[35] *Spirit of Flame*, pp. 25–7.
[36] F. XIII (III, 62).

announced, on that cold February morning, the first thing she saw was the tall figure of Fray Antonio, the former Prior of the Medina monastery, sweeping out the porch, which, as in the second of her own foundations, was used as a chapel.

'How is this, Father!' she called out to him, always full of fun. 'Whatever has become of your reputation?'

Whereupon Fray Antonio looked up, 'with that happy expression which never leaves him.'

'I curse the time,' he replied, 'when I ever had any.'[37]

At Toledo, the primatial city of Spain, Teresa stayed from March to May 1569, and again, for a complete year, from August 1569 to August 1570. It was while breaking her earlier journey thither in Madrid that she first established relations with the King, Philip II, to whom she sent a statement in writing concerning a revelation which she had received about him in a vision. On reading it, Philip was curious enough to ask to see the writer, but, when enquiry was made, it was found that she had left the capital. The incident is worth recording, since Philip was later to become the friend and protector of the Reform and of its foundress.

Reaching Toledo, with two nuns from St. Joseph's, Ávila, on the eve of Lady Day,[38] St. Teresa was warmly welcomed by the hospitable Doña Luisa, who allowed the three to live in seclusion 'as if we had been in a convent.'[39] The foundation, which was not established until May 14, had been planned while she was working at Valladolid, but delay was caused by difficulty in getting a licence and by the conditions attached to their taking possession of a house bequeathed to them by a sympathizer who had recently died. The licence was obtained first; and, with a characteristically buoyant enthusiasm which for once over-rode her sense of reality, the Saint went off and spent all

[37] F. XIV (III, 66). Cf. *Spirit of Flame*, p. 29.
[38] F. XV (III, 70). Cf. LL. 15.
[39] *Ibid.*

the money she had on 'two paintings ... to put behind the altar, two mattresses and a blanket.'[40] And as yet they had no house to keep them in! 'For nearly three months,' she records, 'or at least for more than two—I cannot remember exactly—rich people had been going all over Toledo looking for a house, and they could no more find one than if there were not a single house in the city.[41] Eventually, through the efforts of a young man recommended to them by one of Teresa's Franciscan friends, they succeeded. This youth was 'not at all rich, indeed very poor,' and, she remarks, rather primly, 'his dress was not that of a person with whom Discalced nuns should have anything to do.'[42] Yet, notwithstanding this enigmatic disqualification, he produced a house, of which he brought Teresa the keys, within twenty-four hours. So in they went on the spot, together with the pictures, mattresses and blanket which comprised their entire furniture. Spring comes haltingly to the central Spanish plateau, and at night, lying on the floor, their only covering a single blanket and the frieze capes which they wore over their habits, one can well believe that it was 'rather cold.' Nor had they any fuel— 'not so much as a piece of wood to broil a sardine on'— till some unknown person left them a bundle of sticks.[43] It might be asked what Doña Luisa was about to permit this, and Teresa herself anticipates the question. 'I do not know why it was,' she declares, 'unless God wished us to prove the blessedness of poverty. I did not ask her for anything, as I dislike worrying people, and she may perhaps not have thought of it.'[44] The wealthy are certainly sometimes thoughtless, and Teresa's explanation was, no doubt, the simple, if hardly credible, truth.

It is strange that in so wealthy a city, full of ecclesias-

[40] F. XV (III, 71).
[41] F. XV (III, 72).
[42] F. XV (III, 72).
[43] F. XV (III, 74).
[44] F. XV (III, 74).

tical interests, the Reform should have had such an uphill fight. But Teresa and her companions were not dismayed by it. When, in fact, before very long, gifts started to crowd upon them, the three nuns, who had genuinely been rejoicing in holy poverty, hardly knew where they were. Seeing her companions look sad, she asked them what was the matter.

'What do you think is the matter, Mother?' they replied. 'We do not seem to be poor any longer.'[45]

One of the most curious stories of St. Teresa's foundations concerns her convent at Pastrana. This little town, situated in the extreme south of the province of Guadalajara, had, until a generation before, belonged to the military-religious Order of Calatrava, but was now the property of Ruy Gómez de Silva, one of the most prominent favourites of Philip II, generally known by his title of Prince of Éboli. The Prince's charming but somewhat possessive and erratic wife had for some time been interested in St. Teresa, possibly because of the magnetic attraction which one strong personality is apt to exercise upon another, and there had been some discussion between them as to her making a foundation at Pastrana. Teresa, as we saw at Malagón, had no liking for the idea of convents financed by wealthy individuals, and therefore, humanly speaking, dependent upon them, and she was not too well pleased, exactly a fortnight after the Toledo house had been founded, to receive by letter a rather peremptory summons from the Princess to visit her. Her first impulse was to refuse: the Toledo foundation was so young that it could hardly be left with any safety, and, as the remainder of the nuns who were to live in it had only just arrived, the community life was not yet properly established.[46]

This Teresa explained to the messenger—'a very honest fellow'—who made so bold as to warn her that the Prin-

45 F. XV (III, 75).
46 F. XVII (III, 79).

cess would not brook a refusal, especially as she had gone to Pastrana solely with this idea in mind. So Teresa, anxious as ever to please, and shrewd enough to foresee that the support of Ruy Gómez might one day be invaluable to her, gave the matter further consideration and decided to comply.[47]

She took her time about it, however, not leaving until two days later and spending a week at a Franciscan convent in Madrid. There she was introduced to a hermit who had heard of her Reform and was anxious to join it: by a curious chance, he too had been in touch with the Prince of Éboli, who had promised him a house which he would be willing to hand over to the Carmelite Reform for its second monastery. As St. Teresa had been given patents for two monasteries by her General, and had founded only one, this suggestion seemed to fit in with her plans very well.[48]

When she arrived at Pastrana, she found her would-be patroness in a warm and expansive mood, but also in a somewhat dictatorial one. All kinds of modifications, she said, must be made in the new house before it would be acceptable to her. Teresa met her as far as she could, but some of the requests ran clean contrary to the spirit of the Order, so she 'resolved to go away without making the foundation' rather than comply with them. Eventually, the Prince tactfully 'persuaded his wife to modify her demands'[49] and the convent and the monastery were duly founded, in the second week of July.

Four years later, this story had a sequel, which might be called unexpected, if that adjective were ever applicable to an action of the temperamental Princess. Ruy Gómez died, and his inconsolable wife insisted upon ending her days as a Pastrana nun, demanding special rooms for herself and privileges which no religious Order could give. Teresa

[47] F. XVI (III, 80).
[48] F. XVII (III, 83). Cf. *Spirit of Flame*, p. 32.
[49] F. XVII (III, 84).

reasoned with her, but without success, and eventually she left the convent for a house near by, her thwarted pride taking its revenge by depriving the foundation of the financial support which her husband had guaranteed it on its establishment.[50] As a result, Teresa had it transferred to Segovia, and it was incorporated in a foundation made there in 1574.

VI

FROM SALAMANCA TO SEVILLE: THE *EXCLAMATIONS* AND *CONCEPTIONS* (1570–1575)

ONLY a week after the foundation of the Pastrana monastery, St. Teresa went back to Toledo, so concerned was she for the convent which she had established there under such difficult conditions. She stayed for a full year, until August 1570. Accustomed though she was to the harsh climate of Ávila, the milder air of Toledo seemed to suit her. 'I have been much better this winter,' she wrote in January, 'for the climate in these parts is admirable. . . . I do not believe I have been so well for forty years.'[1]

There is no doubt, I think, that we owe to this period a very beautiful little work called *Exclamations of the Soul to God*.[2] The evidence comes from so serious a scholar as Fray Luis de León, who first published it in the *editio princeps* (1588) of St. Teresa's writings. Fray Luis is quite definite: 'Exclamations, or meditations of the soul to its God,' runs the heading, 'written by Mother Teresa of Jesus, on different days, according to the spirit communicated to

[50] F. XVII (III, 85–6).
[1] LL. 19 (January 17, 1570).
[2] C.W. II, 400–20.

her by Our Lord after she had made her Communion, in the year 1569.' Unless, as some critics have supposed, there is a misprint in the date, that seems final.

The only reason for doubting it is the intense fervour of the seventeen short meditations, which one might be more inclined to connect with St. Teresa's last years. In the Spanish they have a rhythmical quality rare in her work, but this may be attributable, not to maturity of style, but to the fact that the author was setting down words which had actually come from her lips, to be repeated by her again and again and not written to be read by others. Nor does there seem to be any internal evidence for a later date: rather the contrary. The chief difference between the earlier and the later of St. Teresa's mystical works is in the greater depth of her experience after about the year 1572, in which she is generally believed to have first known the Spiritual Marriage. Now in the *Exclamations* there is no suggestion of that state of 'quiet and calm'[3] which the Marriage brings; there is a restlessness, a striving, which might even be considered inconsistent with it. Above all, there is no suggestion of one to whom it is indifferent whether she lives or dies:[4] on the contrary, there is a passionate longing for death, such as both St. Teresa and St. John of the Cross expressed in their verses on the theme:

> *I live, yet no true life I knew,*
> *And, living thus expectantly,*
> *I die because I do not die.*[5]

That is perhaps the dominant theme of the *Exclamations*, which begins with the words: 'O life, life, where canst thou find thy sustenance when thou art absent from thy Life?'[6] and continues:

[3] R. VI (I, 334). Cf. p. 61, n. 54, above.
[4] R. VI (I, 335).
[5] *Poems*, I (III, 277). Cf. *Complete Works of St. John of the Cross*, London, 1934–5, II, 450–1.
[6] *Exclamations*, I (II, 402).

O my Joy, Lord of all things created and my God! How long must I wait before I shall see Thy Presence? What help canst Thou give to one who has so little on earth wherein she can find repose apart from Thee? O long life! O grievous life! O life which is no life at all! Oh, what utter, what helpless loneliness! When shall it end?[7]

So we may, I think, with reasonable confidence, imagine the Saint penning these meditations during her year at Toledo, and later having copies of them made for her daughters. And fortunate it is that she did, since the autograph is lost.

It would be well if the *Exclamations* were re-published as a post-Communion manual for modern readers. Hardly any changes would need to be made in it: hardly a line in it dates. It has much greater unity than the author's other devotional opuscules—the chapters on the Waters in the *Life*, the *Conceptions of the Love of God*, the exposition of the Lord's Prayer in the *Way of Perfection*. Stylistically, it has a curious trick, not uncommon in Spanish, of emphasizing words and phrases by repeating them. Its images are few and commonplace—wars, storms, fire and water, the Divine Eagle—and it contains nothing that can be called expository. To quote P. Silverio, it is a collection of 'white-hot embers from the fire of the Saint's love, which, despite the centuries that have passed since they were first written in the sacred moments after her Communions, can still enkindle the hearts of those who read them.'[8] It is significant that, from the first occasion of their inclusion in St. Teresa's works, they have been placed next to the *Interior Castle*. No more eloquent panegyric could be pronounced upon them.

On All Saints' Day, 1570, Teresa founded her seventh convent, at Salamanca. Considering the reputation held in the sixteenth century by this famous university and cathedral city, and also its nearness to Ávila, one might have

[7] *Exclamations*, VI (II, 406–7).
[8] C.W. II, 400.

expected her to have established her Reform there earlier. She herself explains her failure to do so by the city's poverty, and consequent inability to support another convent founded without means. A request for such a foundation, however, coming from the Rector of the Salamanca house of the Society of Jesus, to which her debts were so great, decided her that this reason was no longer valid: 'When I considered that Ávila is just as poor and God never fails us ... I resolved to make the foundation, providing for it as reasonably as I could.'[9] Without the slightest difficulty a licence was obtained from the Ordinary; a house was rented, though with a little more trouble; and finally, with a single nun, older than herself, as her companion, Teresa went there to take possession. As soon as the foundation was made, more nuns were to come there from the neighbouring town of Medina.[10] It was a cheerless journey, and for some reason they did a large part of it by night. 'It was extremely cold,' Teresa records, 'and I was very poorly in the place where we slept.'[11]

It was noon, on All Saints' Eve (October 31), when Teresa and old María del Sacramento reached Salamanca. Not till nightfall did they get into the house; and, as it had been occupied by students, who, remarks Teresa mildly, 'were not very careful people,' it was in such a state that she had once more to work all night in order to make it fit for Mass on the following morning. After a long and trying journey, a night's hard work and a day's activity, one would have supposed that by the second night the two would have been too weary to do anything but lie down and sleep. Teresa, indeed, was, but not María. About that night, says Teresa, in her *Foundations*, 'I will tell you one thing, sisters, which makes me inclined to laugh.'[12] As we

[9] F. XVIII (III, 86).
[10] F. XIX (III, 93).
[11] F. XVIII (III, 87).
[12] F. XIX (III, 93).

have seen, Teresa could laugh very readily and gaily. This is the story of what amused her.

The house was a large and spacious one—too big, no doubt, for their immediate needs, as well as being 'damp and cold'[13]—and the unfortunate María could not rid her mind of the idea that some of the students might be hiding there. So Teresa selected one of the rooms, laid down the straw which was to be their bed, spread some borrowed blankets to cover them and locked the door. This made her apprehensive companion 'somewhat calmer about the students,' yet still 'she did nothing but look first in one direction and then in the other, all the time with great fear.'

'What are you looking for?' asked Teresa at last, perhaps a little impatiently.

'Mother,' she whispered, 'I am wondering what you would do all alone if I were to die here.'

It was a lugubrious picture, and the constant tolling of the bells of Salamanca's numerous churches (for it was the vigil of All Souls) added to its realism. 'It made me reflect for a moment,' reports Teresa, 'and even frightened me a little; for, though I am not afraid of dead bodies, the sight of them always affects my heart, even when I am not alone.' But in a moment she had recovered; and this was her very sensible answer:

'Sister, if that happens, I shall think what is to be done: for the moment, let me go to sleep.'[14]

Despite numerous setbacks, the Salamancan community flourished, though the size and darkness of the house necessitated a transference three years later. And the account which St. Teresa gives of the new installation reminds us once more how much the fortunes of the Reform had improved since the early days at Ávila and Medina. No hole-in-the-corner inaugurations now: 'There was a large congregation, and we had music, and the Most Holy

13 F. XIX (III, 95).
14 F. XIX (III, 94).

Sacrament was reserved with great solemnity; and, as the house was in a good situation, people got to hear of it and began to esteem it highly.'[15] True, on the very next day, the man who had sold them the house came round and rather disconcertingly demanded the purchase price on the nail—which, apparently, had not been in the bargain; but that was merely because the house had belonged to his wife and she needed the money for her two daughters. In all essentials, St. Teresa records, the community was happy. They were not even troubled by their inability to meet the owner's demands and the consequent prospect of being ejected from the house at short notice: 'Indeed, it is a great pleasure for us to find ourselves in a house from which we may at any time be turned out, when we remember that the Lord of the world had no house at all.'[16]

For the next twelve months Teresa was to move about more than she had ever done before, and this sudden quickening of her activities will perhaps be the most suitable point for an attempt at reconstructing the conditions under which she journeyed. From herself alone we can form some idea of the trials of those expeditions: heat and cold, floods and snow—'there were times when it did not stop snowing the whole day long; others when we lost our way; and others when we had to contend with numerous indispositions and fevers.'[17] In the *Foundations*, as a rule, she says little of the general conditions of her life on tour, though some of the circumstantial accounts of individual journeys lay hold on the imagination. Stray allusions in her letters are equally revealing. But there are also some excellent objective accounts of the routine of those journeys, written by persons who actually shared them, such as the faithful chaplain Julián de Ávila, who accompanied the Saint almost everywhere, Gracián, who also went with her from time to time, María de San José, the Sevilian prioress,

15 F. XIX (III, 96).
16 F. XIX (III, 97).
17 F. XVIII (III, 87).

a talented writer, and the lay sister, Ana de San Bartolomé, who was to be with her at her end.

From these[18] we learn how the Saint was the life and soul of every party—which consisted, as a rule, of three friars, a number of laymen and the nuns who were to form the nucleus of the new community. She at once became the Mother of any group of religious with which she might be travelling and she would make herself responsible for more than their spiritual welfare:

> She encouraged us every one with her profitable and delightful conversation. Sometimes she would speak of the weightiest subjects; at other times she would say things for our entertainment; sometimes, again, she would make up verses, and very good ones, for she was most skilful at this, but she did it only when she found her material ready to hand. So her devotion to prayer did not hinder our spiritual intercourse with her from being friendly and beneficial both to the soul and to the body.

Healthy fun, then, was the rule in the Mother's company: she once told Ana that she disliked 'gloomy people' and she has left on record a prayer to be delivered from 'frowning saints.' At the same time, her fellow travellers were never allowed to forget that they were about their Father's business. Canvas partitions secured the nuns' enclosure, and, as far as possible, says Ana, the daily round was identical with that of the convent. First came Mass and Communion—'which, however hurried they were, was never omitted.' The hours for prayer, self-examination and recitation of the Divine Office were fixed by a travelling clock and announced by the ringing of a little bell; as soon as the bell rang, everyone, including the voluble and loud-voiced drivers and muleteers, 'knew that they must be quiet.' It can be imagined how impatiently the unfortunate men would await the end of the period of prayer or silence.

---

[18] Except where the contrary is stated, in this and the next four paragraphs, quotations are from C.W. III, xii–xv, where the authors are named.

It was wonderful to see how delighted they were at being able to
speak again; and the Saint was always careful at these times to
give them something to eat, as a reward for being so good in
keeping silence.

When they approached an inn where they were to spend
the night, Mother Teresa would send some member of the
party on ahead to arrange for their accommodation,
'asking preferably for large rooms, to take two or three
people each, so that they could all be near together.' Once
installed, one of the nuns would shut the door of their
room and 'act as portress with as much circumspection as
though they were in the convent.' But sometimes the
accommodation was so primitive that the rooms had no
doors and the Mother would then tell off some of the men
to stand outside the entrance till blankets had been fetched
from the carriages to serve as door-curtains.

Of discomforts which combined with those of the
weather to make her journeyings 'one of the most fatiguing
parts of my life and my heaviest trial,'[19] St. Teresa says
little. Some of her companions, however, are less reticent.
To a Saint who, as she herself tells us, loved neatness and
cleanliness almost to excess, the filthy condition of many
of the inns was sheer torture. The frequent noisy quarrels
and fights which would take place at nights were hardly
less unpleasant. Even the ordinary shouting, swearing,
singing and music-making of the rough crowds on holidays
and at festival-times would be trying to women whose
whole lives had been spent in the cloister.

And yet, writes Gracián, in words more expressive than
all the eulogies of hagiographers, anyone who travelled
with the holy Mother would have said she might have been
going about on mules all her life.

In January 1571, Teresa founded her eighth convent, at
Alba de Tormes, fifteen miles from Salamanca, where,
eleven years later, she was to breathe her last. In February,

[19] LL. 70 (January 6, 1575).

she left Alba for Salamanca; in May, she visited St. Joseph's, Ávila; in June, we find her at Medina del Campo; in mid-July, at Ávila again. From August to October, she went back to Medina, as acting-Prioress, and on October 6 she returned to Ávila once more. If Sega, the hostile Nuncio who was to dub her a 'gad-about' (*andariega*), had had these months in mind he might almost have been pardoned. Not that, one imagines, she enjoyed it! 'Again and again,' she wrote once, 'I have thought how much better I should be if I could stay quietly at home.'[20]

But in October 1571 a great and surprising change came over her life and for three years she had very little opportunity to 'gad about' anywhere. For some time there had been trouble at her original convent of the Incarnation. For one thing, the nuns had hardly enough to eat, for which reason the novitiate had been closed by order of the General. Ill-disciplined as they were, many of the 'ladies' began to talk of asking for their freedom and returning to the life of the world. So bad had things become that the Apostolic Visitor could think of only one way to improve them. The nun who had incurred such hard words and such ridicule in the convent when she had founded her Reform nine years earlier had now given ample proof of her genius. She must be brought back to the Incarnation, as its Prioress.

The Reform being still subject to the discipline of the Observance, this was a perfectly practicable, if rather an extraordinary, proceeding, and it will be remembered that Teresa had once previously feared it might happen. Her feelings now can well be imagined. Election would mean that for three years her eight young foundations would remain practically untended. She must leave the tranquillity and the bracing climate of Mount Carmel for the enervating atmosphere of the noisy plain. She must expect to find opposition, perhaps rebelliousness, of a type that she

[20] LL. 70 (January 6, 1575).

had never previously had to contend with. And she was no longer young: fifty-six was a considerable age for a woman in the sixteenth century, and when her term of office was over she would be but a few months short of sixty.

Nevertheless, after signing a solemn undertaking to keep the Reformed Rule all her life, she went—and went to an ordeal which may have been worse even than she had imagined. For many of the wayward and discontented nuns of the Incarnation had no wish to be governed by one who had left them in order to live more strictly. When, accompanied by the Provincial, she entered the choir, an angry group attempted to bar her way. Some cried out against her; others for her. The pandemonium was increased when some of her supporters attempted to sing the *Te Deum* and the rest shouted them down. Teresa took no notice. After kneeling in prayer before the Altar she advanced and faced them. As she stood there the noise subsided and for the first time she addressed the hundred and thirty nuns she was to rule. The purport of her address has come down to us, though not its exact words. It was probably very similar to the address which she made to the nuns at her first Chapter,[21] and of which the humility, courage and absolute freedom from any kind of affectation hardly need emphasis:

> My ladies, mothers and sisters: Our Lord has sent me to this house, by virtue of obedience, to hold this office, which I had never thought of and which I am far from deserving.
>
> This election has greatly distressed me, both because it has laid upon me a task which I shall be unable to perform, and also because it has deprived you of the freedom of election which you used to enjoy and given you a prioress whom you have not chosen at your will and pleasure, and a prioress who would be accomplishing a great deal if she could succeed in learning from the least of you here all the good that is in her.
>
> I come solely to serve and please you in every possible way that I can and I hope that the Lord will greatly assist me to do this—in other respects I could be instructed and improved by anybody. See, then, my ladies, what I can do for each of you; even if

21 Reproduced in C.W. III, 337–8.

it be to give my life-blood, I shall do it with a right good will.

I am a daughter of this house and a sister of you all. I know the character and the needs of you all, or, at least, of the majority of you, so there will be no necessity for you to make a stranger of a person who is so eminently one of yourselves.

Have no misgivings as to how I shall govern you, for though I have thus far lived among and governed nuns who are Discalced, I know well, through the Lord's goodness, the way to govern those who are not. My desire is that we should all serve the Lord in quietness and do the little which our Rule and Constitutions command us for the love of that Lord to Whom we owe so much. I know well how very weak we are; but, if we cannot attain in deed, let us attain in desire. For the Lord is compassionate and will see to it that gradually our deeds become commensurate with our desires and intentions.

In *Spirit of Flame* I have shown how St. John of the Cross enters this three-year picture.[22] It can be imagined how much it meant to St. Teresa when in the following summer he came to the Incarnation as confessor. In several of her letters she refers to the great good that he did there.[23] He remained for more than the whole of her term of office—for over five years, in fact, for it was in December 1577 that he was kidnapped by the friars of the Observance and imprisoned at Toledo. We may be sure that his exacting ideals infused into that convent of the Observance some of the spirit of the Reform and that his presence ensured the continuance of St. Teresa's discipline after her departure.

At some time between April 1571 and May 1575,[24] and therefore most probably during her three years at the Incarnation, when she was free from the exigences of travelling and when she testified that her soul 'seems not to be restless in spite of all this Babel (*Babilonia*),'[25] St. Teresa wrote one of the best known of her shorter works, the *Conceptions of the Love of God upon certain words*

[22] *Spirit of Flame*, pp. 33–5.
[23] LL. 39, 42, 43 (September 27, 1572; February 13, 1573; March, 1573).
[24] The date is discussed in C.W. II, 353–4. The text of the opuscule will be found in II, 357–99.
[25] LL. 31 (November 7, 1571).

of the 'Song of Solomon.' Ostensibly a devotional commentary upon Canticles i, 1–2 and ii, 3–5, its seven chapters roam discursively over a wide field, and, but for the quite decisive tone of the concluding paragraph, one might suppose it to have been the rough draft of some never-completed work written rapidly while the author had the ideas fresh in her mind.

Hoornaert professes to see in the book a plan similar to that of the *Way of Perfection*. The first three chapters, he says, are ascetic, while the remaining four deal in turn with the Prayer of Quiet, the Prayer of Union, ecstasy and the Spiritual Marriage.[26] In reality, the first chapter discusses the Song of Songs in general and its opening verse in particular; the second—by far the longest of the seven—leaves this subject entirely in order to describe 'nine kinds of false peace,' with special reference to life in convents of the Reform; and the third, making only the briefest reference to the Song of Songs, 'treats of the true peace which God grants to the soul, of His union with it and of the examples of heroic charity given by certain of God's servants.' Chapter IV takes a new verse from the Song of Songs and applies it to Quiet and Union: Chapters V and VI treat, somewhat more vaguely, the subject of Union; and Chapter VII deals with several related themes, such as the soul's desire for suffering and the obligations of the contemplative to his neighbour. I cannot see any reference to the Spiritual Marriage; the 'Union' which the Saint describes seems to be conceived in terms of her earlier experiences rather than of her later.

On the whole, this strikes me as the weakest of St. Teresa's works, both in subject-matter and in expression. Being hers, of course, it has its characteristic sallies and its fine moments. I wonder if a single other devotional writer in sixteenth-century Spain would have been bold enough to relate the story of the preacher who tried to describe the

[26] *St. Teresa in Her Writings,* London, 1931, p. 245.

joys of Christ's Bride, 'and the people laughed ... and completely misinterpreted what he said, for he was speaking of love. . . . They simply could not understand it and I believe they really thought he was making it up out of his own head.'[27] 'I know some people who are like them,' adds St. Teresa. So do I; and so will anyone who writes or lectures on the mystics. But, of all the mystics I know, only St. Teresa could have told that story and made that comment. As nearly always, she is just talking intimately to her nuns: 'I like telling you about my meditations, as you are my daughters, although I may be saying a lot of stupid things.'[28] The entire book is stamped with her authentic seal.

Again, in that long second chapter there are some notable passages, containing wholesome instruction, well seasoned with common-sense, on such themes as riches, friendship and discipline. The images of the book are comparatively few and incline to triteness, but a striking exception is a re-treatment of the figure of the child at its mother's breast, first introduced in the *Way of Perfection*. Another characteristic of the *Conceptions* is its frank expression of the 'great joy' which the Saint derives from reading the Song of Songs and 'the Psalms of the glorious King David.'[29] This may be placed beside her testimony in the *Way of Perfection* that she has 'always been fond of the words of the Gospels' and has 'found more recollection in them than in the most carefully planned books,'[30] and beside many other passages in her writings which tell of her devotion to the Bible.[31]

In this instance, however, her affection for the Song of Songs had an unfortunate sequel. That book was very much in the news just then: in 1572, for example, her

[27] *Conceptions*, I (II, 360–1).
[28] *Op. cit.* (II, 362).
[29] *Ibid.* (II, 359).
[30] W.P. XXI (II, 90).
[31] Cf. *Studies*, I, 224–5 and C.W. I, 161.

future editor, Fray Luis de León, had been arrested by the Inquisition (though eventually he was acquitted) on charges of which one of the chief was having translated it into the vernacular. What, then, would the Inquisition say if it heard that a woman—not a priest or a professor or a theologian, but a *woman!*—had dared to write a commentary on it? St. Teresa's confessor, whoever he may have been, had given her leave to do this, but not everyone would have thought it safe, and when in 1574 the Saint came to make a foundation at Segovia, and brought the manuscript with her, the Dominican theologian, Fray Diego de Yanguas, her confessor there, was scandalized. So, as María de San José tersely puts it, he 'ordered it to be burned, because it did not seem suitable to him that a woman should write on the *Songs*. And she obeyed immediately, without questioning his decision.'[32]

Afterwards, continues the writer, Fray Diego 'regretted what he had done,' and we may be sure that his action was purely precautionary. Very possibly he was influenced by the delation of the *Life*, which took place at about that time,[33] and certainly he was aware that many copies of the opuscule, not in its author's handwriting, were in circulation, so that there was no fear of its being lost. An interesting postscript to the affair is that when Fray Luis de León came to edit St. Teresa's writings, after her death, he was still mindful enough of his experiences in the Inquisition's dungeons to omit the *Conceptions*, so it did not appear in print until 1611, when it was edited by Gracián.

Both contemporary testimony and the narrative of her life show that, after an uphill fight, St. Teresa restored discipline to the Incarnation, and also its former prosperity. No doubt she acquired prestige among the nuns from such incidents as that of the intellectual vision which came to her in choir, three months after her arrival, when she

[32] C.W. II, 354.
[33] Cf. p. 49, above.

'saw the Mother of God, with a great multitude of angels, descend to the Prioress's stall ... and seat herself there'[34] —an event still commemorated in the convent annually. But chiefly, we may be sure, the reforms were attributable to her business-like instincts, her determination and her sanctity. After only five months she could describe the nuns as 'placid and good,' and exclaim, 'The Lord be praised for the change He has wrought in them! Even those who were the most stubborn are more contented now and behave better to me.'[35] Still, from the numerous letters with which she relieved her feelings at this time we can glimpse some of the strain behind it all. 'If I had not better health than usual,' she writes to her old friend, Doña Luisa de la Cerda,

I could not possibly bear it.... I don't know how anyone who has known the peace of our houses could live in this turmoil.... You can imagine what trouble it costs to put things right in a house of a hundred and thirty.[36]

Stern discipline and stern economy gradually brought things back to normal, and, by August 1573, victorious but physically exhausted,[37] the Prioress was able to make an extended visit to Salamanca for the transference of the convent there from its great barracks of a house to another more suitable. She stayed until January 1574, (during which period she wrote the first nine chapters of the *Foundations*), and then spent some time at Alba and Medina, before returning home. A few weeks later, she undertook a fresh journey to Segovia, where, on St. Joseph's Day (March 19), 1574, she made her ninth foundation, and, after transferring the Pastrana nuns there during Holy Week, remained, watering the seed she had sown, until the last day of September.[38] On returning to Ávila, she relinquished her office at the Incarnation and

[34] January 19, 1572. R. XXV (I, 346).
[35] LL. 34 (March 7, 1572).
[36] LL. 31 (November 7, 1571).
[37] LL. 33, 46 (February 4, 1572; July 27, 1573).
[38] F. XXI (III, 104–7).

took the more congenial position of Prioress at her own St. Joseph's.

Her next foundation was made on St. Matthias' Day (February 24), 1575, in the beautifully situated southern village of Beas,[39] a place inseparably associated with the name of St. John of the Cross, who went to stay in the convent after his escape from the Toledo prison three and a half years later.[40] This was the farthest point south to which the Reform had penetrated; and later the extension caused some trouble, because Teresa had not been authorized to make foundations in Andalusia. She explains that she did so in complete ignorance, since Beas was some miles outside the political boundary of Andalusia and she had no idea that it fell within the Andalusian province of her Order.[41] Though during the next twelve months she was to make two more foundations in the South, she never took to the people and was not slow to say so. It was at Seville, apparently, that she saw them at their worst:

I do not get on well with the people here.[42]
The injustice that one finds in these parts, the untruthfulness, the duplicity! They deserve all the evil reputation they have, I assure you.[43]
Oh, the lies that are told here! It is astounding.[44]

But at Beas she was singularly happy in the companionship of that gracious and spiritual personality, Anne of Jesus, whom she took with her to be Prioress and who afterwards made a foundation, as the Mother Foundress's deputy, at Granada, where, as readers of *Spirit of Flame* will remember, she was closely associated with St. John of the Cross.[45]

[39] F. XXII (III, 108).
[40] *Spirit of Flame*, p. 55.
[41] F. XXIV (III, 122). Cf. LL. 74 (June 18, 1575), where she explains this to the General.
[42] LL. 86 (December 26, 1575).
[43] LL. 93 (April 29, 1576).
[44] LL. 94 (May 9, 1576).
[45] *Spirit of Flame*, pp. 69, 78, 79, 82.

It was while St. Teresa was at Beas that she first met the remarkable but ill-fated young Jerónimo Gracián,[46] with whom she was to be on intimate terms until her death and whom she eulogizes in her letters even more warmly than St. John of the Cross. Fray Jerónimo was an able young man of exceptional precocity who had joined the Discalced Reform in 1572, at Pastrana, and had begun his career by receiving the doubtful honour of exceptionally rapid promotion. While still a student at the University, he is said to have deputized for his teachers; at Pastrana, almost on his entry, he was made novice-master; just over fifteen months after joining the Order, he was appointed Apostolic Visitor in Andalusia; and, less than two years later, the Nuncio gave him further authority over all the Discalced houses in Castile. It would have been remarkable if such treatment had not aroused opposition. St. Teresa, however, with whom he had already exchanged several letters, could see nothing but good in him. Various people had spoken well of him to her, but (she says) 'when I began to talk to him . . . he pleased me so much that it seemed to me as if those who had praised him to me hardly knew him at all.'[47]

The two soon parted, often to meet again, but the effect which the charm and apparent saintliness of this young man had on the woman of nearly sixty was almost incredible. When they had to part, she set off, with Father Julián and two other companions, from Seville, where her eleventh foundation was made in May 1575. But she could not put Fray Jerónimo out of her thoughts: young though he was, she felt convinced that God had sent him to her for a counsellor and she must co-operate with him to the utmost of her power. So, after long thought, she determined to take a solemn vow of lifelong obedience to him. The decision was not an easy one: 'I realized that, if I made this promise, I should have no freedom, interior or

[46] F. XXIII (III, 117 ff.). Cf. *Studies*, II, 152–3; *Spirit of Flame*, pp. 38–9.
[47] F. XXIV (III, 122).

exterior, for all the rest of my life. . . . I feel I have never in my life done anything, or made any profession, that caused me more repugnance, save when I left my father's house to become a nun.'[48] Eventually, however, her determination triumphed. Making the sole reservation that the reference was 'only to serious matters,'

> I went down on my knees and promised God to do whatever he ordered me all my life long, so long as it was not against the will of God or against the superiors whom I was already bound to obey.[49]

Several days afterwards she told him what she had done.[50] But there is no evidence that the promise ever subsequently oppressed her. 'Blessed be He,' she exclaims, 'Who has raised up someone to satisfy my needs and thus given me the strength to venture to do this.'[51]

The first result of her new vow was a journey into the heart of Andalusia to make a foundation at Seville. Of herself, she would never have ventured into that *fuego*,[52] but Gracián was 'so anxious' for the house to be founded that, had she refused, she would 'have been full of scruples at failing in obedience.'[53] So, preferring apprehensions to scruples, she went.

The eight-day journey began quite pleasantly. Starting at dawn, to avoid as much as possible of the heat, they climbed the Úbeda hills and enjoyed a magnificent panorama, with the blue Sierra Morena on the horizon. Then, as the sun grew stronger, they halted for the *siesta* in a wood, on the banks of a stream; and St. Teresa could no longer remain with her companions but went a stone's throw away, as St. John of the Cross might have done, to rejoice alone in all this beauty. 'We could hardly drag our

[48] R. XL (I, 355).
[49] R. XL (I, 356).
[50] R. XLI (I, 357).
[51] R. XL (I, 356).
[52] LL. 71, 72 (May 11–12, 1575).
[53] LL. 71 (May 11, 1575).

holy Mother away from it,' writes María de San José of that wood, 'for all the various flowers and the thousands of singing-birds seemed to be losing themselves in giving praise to God.'[54]

But before long the journey became less pleasant. 'The heat was now beginning in earnest,' says Teresa; and, torrid as is their own summer, Castilians can feel incredibly oppressed by the heat of lush and fertile Andalusia in mid-May. The nuns travelled, as usual, in covered carriages, and, though they rested during the hottest midday hours, 'when the sun beat down on the carriages with all its might, going into them was like entering purgatory.[55]

None of Teresa's journeys left a more vivid impression upon herself or her companions, and none have they, between them, described in greater detail. On the way, she fell ill 'with a very high fever' and a 'lethargy' from which her companions were unable to rouse her. 'They threw water over my face,' she reports, 'but the sun made it so warm that it refreshed me very little.'[56]

It can be imagined—at least by those who know the unbeaten tracks of Spain today—what Spanish inns must have been like four hundred years ago, and how little adapted they were to the needs of even the most stoical invalid. At the inn where Teresa decided to make a halt on the first day of her illness she was given

> a little room with a sloping roof and without a window, into which the sun streamed whenever the door was opened.... They made me lie down on a bed, but it was so high in one part and so low in another that I would rather have lain on the floor; I cannot think how I endured it—it seemed to be full of sharp stones.... At last I thought it best to get up, so that we could go on our way, for I preferred to endure the sun in the open air than in that little room.[57]

When they set out again, they still had trials in store.

[54] C.W. III, xiv–xv.
[55] F. XXIV (III, 123).
[56] F. XXIV (III, 124).
[57] F. XXIV (III, 124).

Coming to the broad river Guadalquivir, they crossed it by boat, leaving the carriages to be taken over by a somewhat primitive ferry. But by some mischance the boatmen holding the ferry-rope let go of it and down-stream went the boat with the carriage on it but without either rope or oars. It was already dusk and a strong current made the position desperate. The commotion may be imagined. The boatman and his son, a boy of ten or eleven, fell to shouting. The nuns and their companions fell to prayer. A gentleman living in a neighbouring castle sent servants to help them. But everything depended upon the boat and the current and there was little to be done. At last, to the relief of all, the boat struck a sandbank and remained wedged in it till it could be rescued, after which the carriage was safely towed to the other side of the river. By this time night had fallen, but one of the servants from the castle volunteered to show the party the road and the journey proceeded without further interruption.[58]

When at length they reached their inn, with Teresa still suffering from her fever, the prospect of spending the night in it appalled them. The only room available, writes María de San José, 'had, I think, been last inhabited by pigs, and the ceiling was so low that we could hardly stand upright.' It was crawling with vermin, too: 'we did what we could to improve matters,' but obviously that would not be much. So on the next night, rather than risk a second Andalusian hostelry, they camped out in the flower-strewn fields.

A different kind of mischance next befell them. When at last they reached the city of Córdoba, it was very early in the morning, so they asked if there were a quiet church where they could hear Mass without attracting undue attention. They were directed to one on the far side of the river, where they would be 'quite alone,' but on reaching the bridge found that, before crossing it, carriages must have a licence from the Governor. This, 'as nobody was up,' it took them two hours to obtain, during which time great crowds of people going to and from Mass formed around their closed carriage, speculating upon the identity of its occupants. At last the licence came and the carriage rumbled slowly across the bridge. But alas! At the other end there was a gate too narrow to admit it and the nuns had to exercise their patience still longer. 'They had to saw us a way through, or something of the kind,' wrote Teresa, rather vaguely, 'and this took a long time.' At last they came to the church which was to have been their haven of rest; but, by ill luck, they had arrived on its dedication festival and it was crowded out. There was 'a solemn festival service and a sermon.'[59]

Hearing this, the nuns were all of a flutter. If they alighted here, the multitude pouring into the church (or possibly, if the service should suddenly end, pouring out) would be intrigued beyond words at so unusual a spectacle. Rather than become the centre of such a crowd, Teresa thought it would be better for them to forgo Mass altogether. Her fellow nuns agreed with her: no doubt they were invariably swayed by her strong personality. But Father Julián thought otherwise; and, 'as he was a theologian, we had to defer to his opinion.'[60] So they drove on to a quiet spot where they could alight unobserved, and walked towards the church in a body. Even so, their unusual costumes attracted more attention than they cared for. The throng surged around them, commenting volubly: 'there was such an uproar that you would have thought the church had been invaded by bulls.'[61] Fortunately some unknown person came to their rescue and took them to a side-chapel, shutting the door upon them so that Father Julián could say their Mass in peace and quietness. Still, coming after what they had already gone through, the

[59] F. XXIV (III, 125–6).
[60] F. XXIV (III, 126).
[61] F. XXIV (III, 126).

episode was disconcerting: 'a great shock for me, and for all of us,' writes Teresa, in her whimsical way. 'It must have taken away my fever altogether.'[62]

By the time the little service was over, it was almost midday, and the natural thing would have been for them to find a place where they could rest and have some food. But Teresa had taken a dislike to this inquisitive city and was all for getting out of it; so they drove on at once, and, when the hour for the siesta came, stopped in the cool shade of a convenient bridge. Then they did the rest of the ninety torrid miles between Córdoba and Seville, making a stop at Ecija, the notorious 'Andalusian frying-pan,' and reaching Seville on May 26.[63]

It is to be feared that, by the time St. Teresa came to leave that city, her opinion of the Andalusians was no better than it had been before. Even the Archbishop, it appears, was according to sample. He had written to her several times 'with expressions of great affection'[64] and had seemed so well disposed to the Reform that she had quite assumed his acquiescence in her proposal of a foundation. But, when she arrived, and found the house which had been taken for her all ready, she found also that the Archbishop had refused his licence, for the usual reason that there was no endowment.[65]

Here, indeed, was the culmination of a series of disasters. Destitute of resources and nearly four hundred miles from home, what were the poor nuns to do? 'We had not a farthing over from the expenses of the journey and we had brought nothing whatever with us, except the clothes we had on and a few tunics and hoods, and what we needed for our covering and comfort in the carriages.'[66] However, Teresa had no intention of making the four-hundred-mile

[62] F. XXIV (III, 126).
[63] F. XXIV (III, 126).
[64] F. XXIV (III, 126).
[65] F. XXIV (III, 126–7).
[66] F. XXIV (III, 127).

return journey until the house was founded. Inch by inch, as so often before, she got her way. First, the nuns were allowed to have Mass said in their new house on Trinity Sunday, the permit adding 'that no bell must be rung or indeed installed in the house.' (Though, Teresa remarks parenthetically, 'we had installed one already'!) Then the Archbishop, perhaps intrigued by her persistence, 'kept on sending people' to visit the nuns 'and said he would come himself very soon.'[67]

Next came the Calced Fathers, who for some reason had been very difficult about the matter,[68] to enquire why the foundation had been made, and to them Teresa showed the patents given her by the General, carefully saying nothing of the Archbishop's refusal of the licence, which was apparently kept secret from everybody. Finally, he himself arrived; and Teresa, exercising her well-known charm and following her declared policy of complete frankness with prelates, captivated him almost immediately. 'I told him,' she says bluntly, 'of the trouble he was causing us,' and in the end 'he said I could do just what I liked, and as I liked, and from that time forward he was helpful and kind to us on every possible occasion.'[69]

Even this, however, did not end her troubles. Seville was one of the wealthiest cities in Spain; but, as anyone with a knowledge of the world might have predicted, material help came more slowly than it had done anywhere else. Their house was only rented and they had no means of buying one. Nor did candidates for admission present themselves as they had done elsewhere. Soon Teresa was attacked by a depression not due entirely, she feared, to the Andalusian climate. 'I have never found myself as cowardly in my whole life as I was here. I really did not know myself.'[70]

[67] F. XXIV (III, 128).
[68] LL. 74 (June 18, 1575).
[69] F. XXIV (III, 129). Cf. LL. 76 (July 10, 1575).
[70] F. XXV (III, 129).

Then at last their fortunes turned. One day, when she was praying about the house, Our Lord answered her: 'I have heard you: let Me alone.'[71] The help came through that traditional Spanish fairy-godfather, the man who has made his fortune in the Indies. Teresa's brother Lorenzo had returned to Spain after thirty-four years in Spanish America. With characteristic generosity, he stood surety for the money and superintended the drawing up of the title-deeds. Yet still there were set-backs. The first house they decided upon was found to be unsuitable—fortunately, before the signing of the contract. The second, which in April 1576 they took, was a better one, but the tenants refused them possession, and, for reasons which we can only guess at, some neighbouring Franciscans 'came at once' to urge them 'on no account to move there.'[72] Eventually the tenants left and the nuns went in—by night, however, and 'in great fear' of the friars. In fact, records St. Teresa, 'those who accompanied us said that they thought every shadow they saw was a friar.'

The next trouble was the discovery of a flaw in the title-deeds, and until this was put right in the courts Lorenzo thought it best to take a sudden holiday, since otherwise, as surety, he would have been clapped into gaol.[73] However, all was well that ended well. The irregularity disposed of, Lorenzo returned in time to cope with the workmen, who did the needful repairs while the nuns remained 'shut up in some rooms on the ground floor.' Lorenzo also provided them with food, which nobody else in this inhospitable city seems to have thought of doing save an old Carthusian prior of over eighty, who hailed from Ávila. A chapel was prepared, with 'some very good altars and other devices.' And the Blessed Sacrament was reserved—not 'without any fuss,' as St. Teresa had suggested ('for I am greatly opposed to giving unnecessary trouble'), but

[71] F. XXV (III, 130).
[72] F. XXV (III, 131).
[73] F. XXV (III, 132).

in the presence of the Archbishop himself and with all due solemnity.[74] The Archbishop, completely won over, rose fully to the importance of the occasion. He 'ordered the clergy and several confraternities to be present' and even had the streets decorated. The people came to the ceremony 'in tremendous numbers.' There were 'music and minstrels.' In fact, there were fireworks! 'You can well imagine, my daughters, what joy we had that day.' The saintly Prior, who had relaxed his austere habits so far as to walk in the procession, told Teresa that he had 'never seen such a festival in Seville and considered it to be manifestly the work of God.'[75]

As a postscript, in lighter vein, may be given St. Teresa's graphic account of a 'noteworthy thing' which happened at the conclusion of the festival:

> After many guns and rockets had gone off, and when the procession was over and it was nearly night, the people conceived the idea of letting off more guns, and a little powder caught fire, I do not know how, so that it was a great wonder the person to whom it belonged was not killed. A huge flame leapt up to the top of the cloister, the arches of which were covered with silk hangings which they thought would have been set on fire. But they did not take the least harm: they were crimson and yellow hangings. What I consider most astonishing is that the stone work of the arches below the hangings was blackened with smoke, and yet the hangings above were not touched, as if the fire had not reached them.[76]

Everybody, of course, 'was amazed to see this and the nuns praised the Lord that they would not have to buy more hangings.' Their principal emotion, however, was delight at the discomfiture of the devil, who (so the account ends by declaring)

> must have been so angry at the solemnity with which the festival had been kept and at seeing another house of God that he wanted to have his revenge in some way and His Majesty would not allow it. May He be blessed for ever and ever.[77]

[74] F. XXV (III, 133).
[75] F. XXV (III, 133, 134).
[76] F. XXV (III, 133-4).
[77] Ibid. (III, 134).

VII

PERSECUTION: THE *FOUNDA-TIONS*. THE *INTERIOR CASTLE* (1576–1577)

AFTER a year during which she had suffered worse trials than over any other foundation but St. Joseph's, Ávila, Teresa left Seville on the very day after the inauguration of the new house. Her destination was Toledo, but, as she needed some rest and the heat of the summer was beginning, she decided to stay over Whitsuntide at Malagón.[1]

During this Sevilian year, on New Year's Day, 1576, her twelfth foundation had been made at Caravaca—the first to be made in her absence and also one which gave her very little trouble. But trouble of a very serious kind was coming to her, and to the Reform, from another quarter. For over four years after the Caravaca foundation she was able to make no other. 'The reason for this was the very sudden beginning of the great persecutions which both friars and nuns of the Discalced Reform had to endure and... which almost brought the Reform to an end.'[2]

In May 1575, a General Chapter of the Carmelite Order, held at Piacenza, decreed the suppression of the Reformed houses founded in Andalusia on the ground that the General's licence had been valid only for Castile. In this measure Teresa saw the germ of a strife which, as she believed, could not be ended save by the partition of the Order. As the General had to some extent become alienated from the Reform, Teresa turned from him to another source of authority, His Catholic Majesty, King Philip II. Since that March day in 1569, when Philip had failed to make contact with her in Madrid, she had exchanged

---

[1] F. XXVI (III, 134).
[2] F. XXVIII (III, 149). Cf. *Spirit of Flame*, pp. 38–40.

several letters with him and he had given her a special patent for the foundation of the house at Caravaca. Accordingly, on July 19, 1575, she wrote to him, from Seville, quite frankly expounding her misgivings, begging him to use his influence for the separation of the Discalced from the Observance and suggesting that a suitable provincial for the Discalced would be her beloved Father Gracián.

> I have lived among (the Carmelites) for forty years, and, all things considered, I am quite clear that, unless the Discalced are made into a separate province, and that without delay, serious harm will be done: in fact, I believe it will be impossible for them to go on ... (So) I have made bold to write, entreating Your Majesty, for love of Our Lord and His glorious Mother, to give orders that this be done.[3]

At the beginning of August, Ormaneto, the Papal Nuncio, who was well disposed to the Reform, confirmed Gracián in his post as Provincial of Andalusia, 'to reform all the friars of the Carmelite Order in that province' and also created him Apostolic Commissary for the Reform in Castile. The Mitigation at once sent delegates to Rome to protest against this appointment to the Council, who appointed a Portuguese friar, Father Tostado, to enforce the Piacenza decrees and at the same time struck at the root of the trouble, St. Teresa herself.[4]

Shortly before Christmas, 1575, and a few weeks after Gracián had begun his visitation, St. Teresa received a written order from the General to leave Andalusia for some Castilian convent, and once there, to remain. 'In other words,' as she put it, 'sending me to prison.' And this was the General who, 'not many years since,' when she had begged him to cease ordering her to make more foundations, had replied that he would not do that 'because he wanted me to make as many as I have hairs on my head.'[5]

[3] LL. 77 (July 19, 1575). She had not, in fact, been quite forty years in the Order, but she uses the same phrase as a year later (R. IV: I, 319), so was evidently speaking approximately.
[4] Cf. *Spirit of Flame*, p. 39.
[5] F. XXVII (III, 146).

There are various indications that Teresa, tired as she was, would not have minded ending her days in peace, provided she were doing so in obedience to authority. What hurt her most was that the General, who at first had been so gracious to her and so appreciative of her Reform, had shown his displeasure at the extension of her work to Andalusia, and further, 'without the least reason,'[6] had given credence to all kinds of reports spread about her by her enemies. When her Sevilian troubles were at their height, she wrote him a long letter, respectfully pointing out that his original letter had authorized her to make foundations *en todas partes*—'everywhere'—and protesting her affection for him and her filial submission to his authority. Her daughters, she assured him, 'having no other father,' prayed for him daily and could never thank him enough for having authorized the foundation of their convents, and thus being the source of all their happiness.[7] As for herself:

> For the love of Our Lord Your Honour must realize that I would give nothing for all the Discalced put together by comparison with anything that so much as touches Your Honour's garment.[8]

But her protestations appear to have had little effect. 'Nearly all' the Calced Fathers brought 'gross calumnies and opposition' against her, and the General, 'though a most saintly man,' was 'so much worked upon that he did his utmost to prevent the Discalced Reform from making any further progress.'[9]

St. Teresa did not leave Seville for nearly six months after receiving the General's order, for the simple reason that it was overridden by Gracián—'the Apostolic Visitor whom I was bound to obey.'[10] Bound, not because of her private vow, which had contained a condition-clause

[6] F. XXVII (III, 147).
[7] LL. 74 (June 18, 1575).
[8] *Ibid.*
[9] F. XXVIII (III, 149).
[10] F. XXVIII (III, 149).

protecting her against having to disobey her superiors,[11] but because Gracián's authority, derived through the Nuncio from the Pope, seemed to her higher than that of the General elected by the Order.

Early in 1576 the conflict became sharper. Tostado, armed with his powers from the General, arrived in Spain. A Provincial Chapter, held at La Moraleja, decreed a complete fusion of the two branches of the Order, which meant in effect a suppression of the Reform. And finally, in June 1577, the friendly Nuncio Ormaneto died, and was succeeded by one Felipe Sega, who had been worked upon by the Carmelites of the Observance in Rome and, before ever he left that city, was hopelessly prejudiced against the Reform. 'God seemed to have sent him,' writes Teresa, 'to try us by suffering.'[12] No one does she damn with fainter praise. Most of her descriptions of people she disapproves of she qualifies with a 'though he was a great servant of God.' But of the luckless Sega she writes: 'He was related in some way to the Pope and *must have been* a servant of God, but he began by showing very marked favour to the Calced Friars.'[13]

The new Nuncio started his persecution by 'condemning, imprisoning and exiling those who he thought might resist him.'[14] Meanwhile the Discalced had accepted the challenge and there began the battle of the eagles and the butterflies, as Teresa, in her letters, picturesquely terms the two parties. In August 1576, Father Gracián summoned a Chapter of the Reform at Almodóvar. This refused to accept the decisions of the Moraleja Chapter (at which no Discalced friars had been present) and declared the Discalced a separate province with rules of its own. It also ordered that two friars of the Reform should be sent to Rome, a move which St. Teresa strongly supported:

[11] R. XL (I, 356).
[12] F. XXVIII (III, 150).
[13] *Ibid.* Italics mine.
[14] *Ibid.*

If (the friars of the Observance) give the Pope information which is not true and there is no one there to defend us, they will obtain all the Briefs against us they want. It is most important, therefore, that some of our friars should be there, and then people will see the kind of life they lead, and realize that our enemies are animated by passion. Until this has been accomplished I do not believe we can do anything. Further, our friars would bring back a licence to found more houses. Believe me, it is a great thing to be prepared for anything that may happen.[15]

By this time the King had intervened, appointing four assessors, 'weighty persons, three of them members of religious Orders,' to examine the case with care. One of them, Fray Pedro Fernández, was a Dominican of 'most saintly life, great learning and understanding,' whom Teresa had already known some years earlier as Apostolic Visitor to the Order. 'When I learned that the King had appointed him, I considered the matter as good as settled, as, by the mercy of God, it has been.'[16] It was not, however, to be settled immediately.

We must now rejoin Teresa in Toledo, where she arrived, by way of Malagón, towards the end of June 1576. One of her first tasks was to continue writing her *Foundations*, which she had begun three years earlier, at Salamanca, at the command of her confessor Ripalda—'my great friend in the Society of Jesus.'[17] After writing nine chapters, she had been compelled by her 'numerous occupations' to lay down her pen. By the time more leisure came, she had 'determined not to continue' this raciest of her books, since Ripalda had left the district and she was no longer in touch with him.[18] But Gracián, hearing of this, insisted upon her doing so. She argued with him—'I told him what little opportunity I had for writing'—but he replied that she would have ample time in her enforced seclusion. 'I also told him how tired it made me'[19]—but Gracián knew how

[15] LL. 105 (September 5, 1576). Cf. LL. 111 (September 20, 1576).
[16] F. XXVIII (III, 151).
[17] LL. 147 (December, 1576).
[18] F XXVII (III, 148).
[19] *Ibid.*

to counter that argument too. She could write *poco a poco u como pudiese*: 'a little at a time, or according as she had the opportunity.' This happened about the July of 1576. Teresa, true to her special vow of obedience to Gracián, argued no further, but wrote to her brother in Ávila for the manuscript of the first nine chapters, together with other papers that she would need for writing the rest.[20] Not till October, however, did she start work;[21] and then she made up for lost time. True, one chapter—on the Alba foundation—was among the 'other papers,'[22] but it is astonishing that, after little more than five weeks—by November 14—the nine chapters should have become twenty-seven. The last four chapters, which complete the book, and bring the narrative down to April 19, 1582, were probably written *pari passu* with the events they describe: this is certainly true of the last chapter, on the foundation at Burgos.[23]

It is at this point in her life, when, in better health than for years,[24] she was busily recollecting the events connected with her foundations and feverishly putting them on paper, that we may most appropriately glance at the *Book of the Foundations* as a whole. There is no need to outline the story it tells, since that is being related in these chapters. But there are some interesting and characteristic digressions and something should also be said of the book as a whole.

From the literary standpoint it is, of St. Teresa's five major works, the least commendable. It is easy to read, for

[20] LL. 101 (July 24, 1576).
[21] LL. 115, written to Gracián on October 5, 1576, says, 'Now I *shall begin* the matter of the foundations,' and the context makes it clear that the reference is to this book.
[22] *I e.* Chapter XX. The letter (LL. 101) refers only to 'a paper in which are written certain things about the Alba foundation,' so the chapter may not have been put together in its final form. Cf. C.W. III, xvii.
[23] *Ibid.*
[24] LL. 101.

a foreigner as well as for a Spaniard, and its animation, its chatty, intimate style and its lavishness of homely detail make it particularly attractive. But it rambles to excess. Errors, unconscious omissions and slips of the pen bear witness to the speed at which it was written and in the latter part of the autograph—preserved in excellent condition—the handwriting shows signs of age. Perhaps it is fairest to judge the *Foundations* as one would a series of letters.

It must be owned that, if one of the Saint's major works had to be sacrificed—an idea at which good Teresans will very properly be horrified—it is with the *Foundations* that we should reluctantly have to part. For it is concerned almost entirely with external events, like a conventional autobiography. Contrast, for example, the insight into life in the 'little dovecotes of the Virgin Our Lady'[25] given in parts of the first eight chapters with the corresponding chapters in the *Way of Perfection*. They add a vast amount more detail. There are striking portraits of those earnest souls in the pictures of the 'intelligent and gifted' sister planting the rotten cucumber,[26] of the not so intelligent sister who reported that 'Our Lady often came to her, sat down on her bed and stayed talking with her for more than an hour';[27] of the literal-minded nun who was told by her impatient prioress to 'run away and play' and forthwith did so 'for some hours';[28] and of the exceptionally humourless one who

> brought her Prioress a very large worm, asking her to look and see what a fine specimen it was. The Prioress laughingly said: 'Go and eat it, then.' So she went and fried it. The cook asked her what she was doing and she said that she was going to eat it, which she was in fact about to do. Thus the Prioress' very careless remark might have done her great harm.[29]

[25] F. IV (III, 17).
[26] F. I (III, 2).
[27] F. VIII (III, 43).
[28] F. XVIII (III, 92, n. 1).
[29] F. XVIII (III, 92).

By painful contrast, the chapter on the treatment of nuns with melancholia throws a penetrating light on mental suffering in the sixteenth century.[30] No less illuminating is the picture of 'one of our houses' the Prioress of which

> was greatly attached to penance and made all the nuns lead penitential lives. She would discipline the whole convent at once by ordering the recitation of the seven penitential Psalms, with prayers and other things of that kind. This is what happens if a prioress becomes absorbed in prayer; she makes the whole convent follow her in this, even outside the hours of prayer—after Matins, indeed, when it would be better if the nuns went to sleep. If, however, as I say, she is attached to mortification, there has to be continual activity of this kind, and these little lambs of the Virgin must suffer it in silence, as if they were real lambs.[31]

St. Teresa could be as scathing about prioresses as about confessors, and the advice she gives them in Chapter XVIII shows an immense range in the knowledge of human nature. The few pages on the interior life, on the other hand, though valuable, like everything else St. Teresa wrote, and though not without their illuminating phrases, are elementary, and even thin, by comparison with the *Way of Perfection*.

The digressions are full of charm. 'How far I have wandered from my subject!' exclaims Teresa at the opening of Chapter IX—and she is right, for of the preceding eight chapters only about two and a half have kept to the track. But none of her readers would reproach her for that, and still less do the later digressions offend them. For, after all, this is not a closely knit drama, with its preparation, conflict and *dénouement*, but a book of reminiscences, in which it is perfectly permissible for the author to write about everything in the least connected with her subject. And St. Teresa felt like that about it too. 'I have been making a long digression,' she sighs at the beginning of Chapter XIX. But 'when anything occurs to me which I have learned by the experience which the Lord has given me, it

[30] F. VII (III, 36–40).
[31] F. XVIII (III, 89).

worries me if I cannot discuss it.'[32] And that no doubt explains all those later digressions, which, with great intimacy of detail, with occasional eloquence and with not infrequent humour, tell of some of the outstanding personalities whom Teresa had met.

Personally, I like best the story of eleven-year-old Casilda de Padilla, beneath the *naïveté* of which can be discerned so intense a knowledge of the world, and which is told with amazing zest and vivacity. How graphic are the descriptions of Casilda's two attempts to enter the convent! On the first occasion she goes for a drive, attended by servants, one of whom she tells to call at the convent and ask for a glass of water. This done,

> she got down very quickly from the carriage . . . and when they opened the door slipped inside, embracing the statue of Our Lady, weeping and begging the Prioress not to turn her away. The servants shouted and knocked at the door, but she went to the grille to speak to them and told them that she would never come out again and that they could go and tell her mother.[33]

Mother, grandmother and the uncle to whom her mother had betrothed her came to the convent grille to reason with her, but Casilda had already proved herself expert in the art of answering back. When her mother had told her that she was too young to become a nun she had pertinently enquired why, if she was old enough to be betrothed to a man, she could not be betrothed to Christ. When her sister, who had taken the veil, had painted to her the joys of remaining in the world, she had answered, 'Why, then, did *you* leave it?' And now,

> after much lamentation, her betrothed said to her that she could serve God better by giving alms; but she answered that he could do that himself. To all the other reasons he gave her she replied that . . . there was nothing in her for him to complain of, for she had left him only for God, and in this she was doing him no wrong. When she saw that no argument could convince him she got up and left him.[34]

[32] F. XIX (III, 92).
[33] F. XI (III, 55).
[34] F. X, XI (III, 52, 54, 55).

Not to be beaten, the uncle, pleading her tender years, obtained a Royal Order for her forcible release. After her twelfth birthday, however, she tried again, and this time all went well and she lived happily ever after.

One day, when she was in church, about to hear Mass with her mother, the latter entered a confessional and she asked her companion to go to one of the fathers and beg him to say a Mass for her. When she saw that she had gone, she put her shoes in her sleeves, caught up her skirt and ran with the greatest possible haste to this convent.... Entering by the outer door, she shut it and began to cry out. When her companion arrived, she was already in the convent, where they gave her the habit at once. Thus were fulfilled the good beginnings which the Lord had wrought in her. And soon His Majesty began to reward her with spiritual favours and she to serve Him with the greatest happiness.[35]

No more of these naïve but charming biographical incidents can be related, but the sympathetic reader will derive pleasure as well as profit from the stories of Beatrice of the Incarnation, who suffered from innumerable abscesses but died in peace;[36] Teresa de Laíz, who endowed the Alba convent, despite the warnings of 'two monks ... both very good and learned men,' that 'nuns are as a rule discontented people';[37] saintly Catalina Godínez, who would 'moisten her face and expose it to the sun' to escape offers of marriage;[38] Beatrice of the Mother of God, who had the mysterious vision of a venerable Discalced friar;[39] and the hermit Catalina de Cardona, who signed her letters with the words 'The Sinner.'[40] Despite their varied quaintnesses these stories all ring true; and, if occasionally their pointed reminders of the changes that four centuries have brought make the reader smile, it is certainly not Teresa who will blame him.

[35] F. XI (III, 56–7).
[36] F. XII (III, 57–61).
[37] F. XX (III, 98–101).
[38] F. XXII (III, 109–111).
[39] F. XXVI (III, 135–9).
[40] F. XXVIII (III, 156–62).

At the same time he must remember that the book was not written for him at all. Nothing, probably, would have surprised its author more than to know that it would be widely read by all sorts and conditions of people, living in the world—and all over the world—hundreds of years later. We must always judge a book, or for that matter anything else, in relation to its author's aim; and the aim of this book, given us in its author's own words, explains, not merely its familiar character and its discursive style, but also the abundance of detail into which it enters. Just as the *Life*, St. Teresa's spiritual autobiography, was written exclusively for her confessors, so the *Foundations*, the story of her most active years, and the biography, as it were, of her convents, was written for the inmates of those convents, in order to remind them of the goodliness of their heritage.

> It is well, my daughters, that those of you who read of these foundations should know how much you owe those who made them, so that, since they laboured so hard and so disinterestedly to obtain this blessing which you enjoy of living in one of our houses, you should commend them to Our Lord, and give them whatever advantage there is in your prayers. If you knew what bad nights and days they had endured, and what hardships attended their journeys, you would do this very willingly.[41]

Perhaps the writing of this second instalment of eighteen chapters stimulated Teresa's natural aptitude for self-expression and gave her the desire to produce something of more lasting value. In any case, only six months later she took up her pen again, to write what is by far the profoundest and most deeply spiritual of her longer works, *The Interior Castle*. From three sources—herself, her friend Gracián and her biographer Yepes—we have full information about its conception and birth. She had been talking with Gracián about some spiritual matter which she remembered having treated in her *Life*, the manuscript of

[41] F. XXI (III, 106).

which she had taken the precaution of leaving with the Inquisition.[42]

'Well,' said Gracián, seizing an obvious opportunity, 'as we cannot get at that, why not recall what you can of it, and of other things, and write a fresh book, and expound the teaching in a general way, without saying to whom the things that you describe have happened?'[43]

Following up the impression which he saw he had made, Gracián then suggested that she should talk the matter over with her good friend Dr. Velázquez, who concurred; so she sat down to consider what form the new book should take. Though she had probably not realized it, an idea had been forming in her mind years before while she was writing the *Way of Perfection*—the idea of portraying the interior life as a palace or castle containing numerous 'mansions.' Several phrases which escaped her in that book betrayed the direction which her thoughts were taking:

> I told them that the Lord had different roads by which they might come to Him, just as He also had many mansions.[44]
>
> Those who are able to shut themselves up in this way within this little Heaven of the soul, wherein dwells the Maker of Heaven and earth. . . .[45]
>
> And now let us imagine that we have within us a palace of priceless worth, built entirely of gold and precious stones—a palace, in short, fit for so great a Lord. Imagine that it is partly your doing that this palace should be what it is—and this is really true, for there is no building so beautiful as a soul that is pure and full of virtues, and, the greater these virtues are, the more brilliantly do the stones shine. Imagine that within the palace dwells this great King.[46]

On Trinity Eve, June 1, 1577, these ideas suddenly crystallized into a vivid picture: 'a most beautiful crystal globe, made in the shape of a castle, and containing seven mansions, in the seventh and innermost of which was the

[42] Cf. p. 49, above.
[43] C.W. II, 188–9.
[44] W.P. XX (II, 85).
[45] W.P. XXVIII (II, 115).
[46] W.P. XXVIII (II, 117).

King of Glory, in the greatest splendour, illumining and beautifying them all':

> The nearer one got to the centre, the stronger was the light; outside the palace limits everything was foul, dark and infested with toads, vipers and other venomous creatures. While she was wondering at this beauty, which by God's grace can dwell in the human soul, the light suddenly vanished. Although the King of Glory did not leave the mansions, the crystal globe was plunged into darkness, became as black as coal and emitted an insufferable odour, and the venomous creatures outside the palace boundaries were permitted to enter the castle.[47]

That evening she told Yepes about this vision and on the very next day she sat down to write. The book was composed at a speed which she never equalled before or since. Though interrupted for about three months by business concerning the Order, she had completed it by November 29. Then she entrusted it to Gracián, who sent it to a number of people for perusal and criticism; and, in the June and July of 1580, a committee of three—Teresa, Gracián and the Dominican Yanguas—met to discuss it further at Segovia.[48] During these meetings a few corrections were made. But some years later, many of these were expunged by another critic, probably Ribera, who restored the original text. The book as we have it, therefore, contains substantially what Teresa wrote in those two periods at Toledo and Ávila, totalling barely three months—an achievement, considering the intricacy and profundity of the subject, so remarkable that it is not surprising if many of her admirers, fortified by contemporary testimony that she wrote parts of it in a state of rapture, have thought of it as miraculous. But it will suffice to credit her with the most intense concentration. 'I often saw her as she wrote,' deposes one witness, 'which was generally after Communion. She was very radiant and wrote with great rapidity, and as a rule she was so absorbed in her work that even if

[47] C.W. II, 188.
[48] Cf. p. 153, below.

we made a noise she would never stop, or so much as say that we were disturbing her.'[49]

And the book is what one would expect of a masterpiece written with such intensity. I have already said why I consider it Teresa's greatest. For the same reasons it is the easiest to describe. Its construction is ideally simple and clear, the few digressions, as pertinent as charming, never blurring its outline. 'It is difficult,' a modern commentator has observed, 'to say how far experiential mysticism can ever lend itself to inflexible scientific rule without endangering its own spirit. Since God is free to establish an ineffable communion with the questing soul, the soul must be free to set down its experiences as they occur to it.[50] Such freedom St. Teresa needed, no less to satisfy her inborn spontaneity than because of the nature of her subject, yet she succeeded in combining it with an attention to method which few mystical writers have surpassed.

The *Interior Castle* gives a survey of the contemplative life, in the fuller form in which she had come to know it since beginning her autobiography, and it might therefore be described as an amplification of the chapters on prayer, which constitute, as it were, an opuscule set in the framework of that book. The Mystic Way is represented by the progress from the outer courtyard of the castle to its innermost mansion, 'where the most secret things pass between God and the soul.'[51] The castle is itself the soul,[52] but that seeming paradox presents no difficulty, for 'the kingdom of God is within you.' A more curious idea is that it should have 'many mansions, some above, others below, others at each side,'[53] through which the pilgrim may 'roam about': a conception presumably intended to emphasize a truth of which she never loses sight—that different souls

[49] C.W. II, 196.
[50] P. Silverio. C.W. II, 189.
[51] I.C. I, i (II, 202).
[52] I.C. I, i (II, 203).
[53] I.C. I, i, ii (II, 202, 207–8).

progress towards perfection by different paths, and that the experiences of any one contemplative at a particular stage of his journey are not necessarily identical with those of any other.

These few notes alone will illustrate the superiority of the *Interior Castle* over the opuscule on the Waters. As we follow the pilgrim's progress from the courtyard to the innermost room, this will become still clearer.

Inside the castle all is light, save when mortal sin plunges it into darkness,[54] but the courtyard, infested with 'snakes and vipers and poisonous creatures,'[55] is dark and cold. As the soul knocks at the gateway of vocal prayer and meditation, and seeks an entrance to the First Mansions—those of Humility—these reptiles, which typify worldly distractions, attempt to enter with it, and some of them will probably succeed. Fewer, however, will get into the Second Mansions—of the Practice of Prayer—and fewer still into the Third—of Meditation and Exemplary Life. We saw how, in her earlier treatise, St. Teresa, no doubt with a vivid memory of the shortcomings of her own immaturity, devoted a great part of her space to counselling beginners. So here: in continual contact, as she is, with imperfect souls, the Mother Foundress is too practically minded to write only for those who have already attained, and she devotes a liberal proportion of her longer work to travellers unlikely to go farther than the point at which she has now arrived. In other words, to the First Water—or, in other charts of the *via mystica*, to the Way of Purgation— correspond no less than three of the Mansions. And, notwithstanding the sublimity of the *Interior Castle* as a classic of the mystical life, St. Teresa has written nothing on asceticism more notable or more precious than these early chapters. Most notable are her initial meditation on the dignity of the human soul, her constantly reiterated

[54] I.C. I, ii (II, 205–6).
[55] I.C. I, ii (II, 210).

insistence on humility, her warnings against trusting to one's own strength and her clearly drawn picture of the attainments and the limitations of those who have reached the Third Mansions. More forcefully and less discursively than in the *Way of Perfection*, the Mother is here addressing herself to the generality of her daughters, and at the same time to the rank and file of the great family of Our Lord Jesus.

As he enters the Fourth Mansions the pilgrim sets foot inside those supernatural realms of which he has until now caught only the merest glimpses. The poisonous reptiles have all but gone—or, to put it differently, the shackles which have hindered the pilgrim's progress are broken—and the soul becomes conscious of gaining something otherwise than by its own efforts. And what it gains is the gift of God known as the Prayer of Quiet.

In other words the Fourth Mansions correspond to the Second Water, and, in her attempt at exposition, St. Teresa reverts to her original metaphor. Let us imagine two fountains whose basins are filled in two different ways. 'The water in the one comes from a long distance, by means of numerous conduits and through human skill; but the other has been constructed at the very source of the water and fills without making any noise. If the flow of water is abundant, as in the case we are speaking of, a great stream still runs from it after it has been filled; no skill is necessary here, and no conduits have to be made, for the water is flowing all the time.'[56]

Now the water that comes through the conduits is a 'spiritual sweetness' arising from meditation. We strive to meditate, perhaps at the cost of wearying the mind—and we get our reward. The satisfaction which this mental exercise brings fills the basin of the fountain, 'but in doing so makes a noise.' To the other fountain 'the water comes direct from its source, which is God, and as God wills . . .

[56] I.C. IV, ii (II, 236–7).

with the greatest peace and quietness and sweetness within ourselves.' In fact, it often overflows from the soul into the body.[57]

During the fifteen years which elapsed between her two descriptions of the Prayer of Quiet, St. Teresa's experience had greatly deepened. 'It may be,' she warns us, 'that I am contradicting what I have myself said elsewhere. This is not surprising. . . . Perhaps the Lord has now given me a clearer realization of these matters than I had at first.'[58] Even as early as 1565, in the *Way of Perfection*, she contradicts the statement in the *Life* that the faculties of the soul, in the Prayer of Quiet, are not asleep. In the *Way of Perfection* the Prayer of Quiet is described as a 'swoon,'[59] and in the fifth *Relation* (1576) as a 'sleep of the faculties.' But in the *Interior Castle*, as though unwilling to make any further attempts at definition, she writes more vaguely,[60] and, as before, takes refuge in those incomparable mystical images which no one has used with greater effect.

None the less, the *Interior Castle* breaks new ground in distinguishing a state immediately preceding the Prayer of Quiet—an anteroom, as it were, to the Fourth Mansions— which she calls the Prayer of Recollection. A year previously Teresa had described this, in the fifth *Relation*, as 'the first kind of prayer I experienced which seems to me supernatural . . . one which, despite all our efforts, cannot be acquired by industry or diligence . . . an interior recollection felt in the soul, which . . . sometimes carries the exterior senses away with it.'[61] It is this state that leads into the Prayer of Quiet and 'almost always' (says the *Interior Castle*) precedes it. 'A person involuntarily closes his eyes and desires solitude; and, without the display of any human skill, there seems gradually to be built for him a

[57] I.C. IV, ii (II, 237).
[58] I.C. IV, ii (II, 238).
[59] W.P. XXXI (II, 127).
[60] For a fuller discussion of this point, see *Studies*, I, 170-3.
[61] R. V (I, 327).

temple in which he can make the prayer already described.'[62] Outward things lose their hold, yet meditation and
other activities of the understanding continue. This partition, as it were, of the Fourth Mansions would appear to
resolve the confusion caused by the author's deepening
experience.

The Fifth Mansions, corresponding, with slight varia-
tions, to the Third Water, are commonly known as the
Prayer of Union or the Spiritual Betrothal. Here the soul
is completely asleep to the things of the world, and aban-
dons itself to God, Who, for the time being, takes complete
possession of it. The experience can never be forgotten nor
its reality doubted: 'when the soul returns to itself, it cannot possibly doubt that God has been in it and it has been
in God; . . . although for years God may never grant it that
favour again it cannot forget it.'[63] On the other hand, it is
only a brief experience—lasting 'never, I think, for as long
as half an hour.'[64] It is for this reason that it is called a
'Betrothal' and contrasted with the Seventh Mansions, the
'Marriage.' When two people, says St. Teresa, are con-
templating marriage, they discuss 'whether or no they are
suited to each other and are both in love; and then they
meet again so that they may learn to appreciate each other
better.' So it is here. The meeting 'is over in the very
shortest time,' but 'the soul sees in a secret way Who this
Spouse is that she is to take.'[65]

But St. Teresa's description of the Prayer of Union has
been made famous by another figure than this—perhaps
the most beautiful, and the most fertile, of all the figures
she ever used—the Similitude of the Silkworm. Someone
had told her—she knew nothing of such things herself, 'so
if it is incorrect in any way the fault is not mine'—of 'the
wonderful way in which silk is made—a way which no

[62] I.C. IV, iii (II, 240).
[63] I.C. V, i (III, 251).
[64] I.C. V, ii (III, 255).
[65] I.C. V, iv (II, 264–5).

one could invent but God—and how it comes from a kind
of seed which looks like tiny peppercorns.'[66]

> When the warm weather comes, and the mulberry-trees begin to
> show leaf, this seed starts to take life; until it has this sustenance,
> on which it feeds, it is as dead. The silkworms feed on the
> mulberry-leaves, until they are full-grown, when people put down
> twigs, upon which, with their tiny mouths, they start spinning
> silk, making themselves very tight little cocoons, in which they
> bury themselves. Then, finally, the worm, which was large and
> ugly, comes right out of the cocoon a beautiful white butterfly.[67]

The silkworm is, of course, the contemplative soul,
which feeds upon its mulberry leaves ('the general help
which God gives to us all . . . in His Church') until it is
full-grown, and then starts to 'build the house in which it
is to die,' its life hidden with Christ in God. As the force of
the similitude deepens in her mind, Teresa's emotion
deepens too:

> On, then, my daughters! Let us hasten to perform this task and
> spin this cocoon. Let us renounce our self-love and self-will, and
> our attachment to earthly things. Let us practise penance, prayer,
> mortification, obedience, and all the other good works that you
> know of. . . . Let the silkworm die—let it die, as in fact it does
> when it has completed the work which it was created to do. Then
> we shall see God and shall ourselves be as completely hidden in
> His greatness as is this little worm in its cocoon.[68]

After being 'dead to the world,' and 'hidden in the great-
ness of God,' the silkworm emerges, 'a little white butterfly.' Though 'it has never been quieter or more at rest in its
life,' it appears to be restless.

> By comparison with the abode it has had, everything it sees on
> earth leaves it dissatisfied. . . . It sets no store by the things it did
> when it was a worm. . . . It has wings now. . . . All that it can do
> for God seems to it slight by comparison with its desires. . . .
> Everything (else) wearies it, because it has proved that it can find
> no true rest in the creatures.[69]

[66] I.C. V, ii (II, 253).
[67] I.C. V, ii (II, 253).
[68] I.C. V, ii (II, 254–5).
[69] I.C. V, ii (II, 255–6).

This extended metaphor leads us by a natural sequence of thought into the Sixth Mansions, a kind of 'incipient union' characterized by greater afflictions, and corresponding in some sort with St. John of the Cross's Dark Night of the Spirit. The 'little butterfly' has now no resting-place. 'It cannot return to the place it came from, for, as has been said, however hard we try, this is not in our power.' So it enters upon new trials—but trials 'of such sublimity' that they 'bring peace and contentment.'[70] These trials are described at great length in the sixth of the seven sections of the *Interior Castle*, which is nearly as long as the first five put together. Some of them are wholly external—and these include physical sufferings directly related with spiritual experience; others, the greatest of them, are interior. At times they are almost overwhelming, yet, since they are the wounds of love, they bring the soul joy as well as pain.

A good deal is said in this section about supernormal phenomena, which, from the Fifth Mansions onward, tend to recur. The different types of locution and vision are described in detail, as also are rapture, ecstasy and trance, which in the Sixth Mansions are quite continuous.' Teresa treats them as one and distinguishes from them a 'flight of the spirit'—a transport coming upon the soul with tremendous rapidity and quite irresistibly. Once more she returns to the figure of the Waters to give some impression of its nature. In the Fourth Mansions, she says, the basin of the fountain filled 'gently and quietly—I mean without any movement.'

But now this great God, Who controls the sources of the waters and forbids the sea to move beyond its bounds, has loosed the sources whence water has been coming into this basin; and with tremendous force there rises up so powerful a wave that this little ship—our soul—is lifted up on high. And if a ship can do nothing, and neither the pilot nor any of the crew has any power over it, when the waves make a furious assault upon it and toss it about at their will, even less able is the interior part of the soul to stop

[70] I.C. V, ii (II, 256).

where it likes, while its senses and faculties can do no more than has been commanded them: the exterior senses, however, are quite unaffected by this.[71]

In this transport the soul really seems to leave the body and the subject to have visited another region, 'very different from this in which we live, and has been shown a fresh light there, so much unlike any to be found in this life that, if he had been imagining it, and similar things, all his life long, it would have been impossible for him to obtain any idea of them. In a single instant, he is taught so many things all at once that, if he were to labour for years on end in trying to fit them all into his imagination and thought, he could not succeed with a thousandth part of them.'[72]

These are some of the sublime themes touched upon in the chapters which describe the Sixth Mansions and are among the most remarkable that St. Teresa ever wrote. For not only does she soar high in them, and yet write with a sureness of touch which could only be the result of genuine experience, but at the same time she remains her ever practical self and keeps in mind those who habitually live on a low level while striving after a higher. No better illustration than these chapters can be found of the description of the Castilian as one with feet firmly planted on the soil yet with gaze fixed on Heaven.

At last, in the Seventh Mansions, St. Teresa conducts us into the innermost chamber of the King and tells us something of that most sublime and intimate of all human experiences, the Spiritual Marriage. In the innermost chamber 'His Majesty alone dwells'; it may be called a 'second Heaven.'[73] The pilgrim is led into it by an intellectual vision in which all three Persons of the Most Holy Trinity reveal Themselves to him, in an illumination which penetrates his spirit like a cloud of the most dazzling

[71] I.C. VI, v (II, 293–4).
[72] I.C. VI, v (II, 295).
[73] I.C. VII, i (II, 330).

light.[74] The union which follows takes place 'in the centre of the soul,'[75] and, most important of all, it is not a fleeting experience, like the Betrothal, which 'passes quickly, and afterwards the soul is deprived of that companionship—I mean so far as it can understand.'[76] With only the briefest intervals,[77] the Marriage is a state of permanent peace.

Many years before, as a child, Teresa had loved to dwell on the words *para siempre*—'for ever—ever—ever.' In these last years of her life she had her first realization of their meaning. In the *Life*, the Fourth Water is an experience of brief duration differing but little from the Third and equivalent to the Spiritual Betrothal. But the Seventh Mansion, the Marriage, is *para siempre*.[78] There is the same difference between the two as there is 'between two betrothed persons and two who are united so that they cannot be separated any more.[79] There is even incorporation (the soul is 'made one with God'[80] and indissolubility ('they have become like two who cannot be separated from one another'[81]).

Even St. John of the Cross, a university man, trained in the art of writing, found such conceptions difficult to put into words. To St. Teresa, with no less rich a store of experience and fewer words in which to express it, the task was appalling. Once again, she seeks a way out through similitudes. The Marriage is like

> rain falling from the heavens into a river or a spring; there is nothing but water there and it is impossible to divide or separate the water belonging to the river from that which fell from the heavens. Or it is as if a tiny streamlet enters the sea, from which

[74] I.C. VII, i (II, 331).
[75] I.C. VII, ii (II, 334).
[76] I.C. VII, ii (II, 335).
[77] I.C. VII, iv (II, 344).
[78] I.C. VII, ii (II, 335).
[79] I.C. VII, ii (II, 334).
[80] I.C. VII, ii (II, 335).
[81] I.C. VII, ii (II, 335).

it will find no way of separating itself, or as if in a room there were two large windows through which the light streamed in: it enters in different places but it all becomes one.[82]

Those in the innermost Mansions now have few raptures and less violent ones than in the past. They still have trials, but never lose their peace: 'the few storms pass quickly, like waves of the sea, and fair weather returns, and then the Presence of the Lord which they have within them makes them forget everything.'[83] Even the desire to die and be with Christ, previously so insistent and overwhelming, is now gone: all that the soul wishes for is God's will, whatever that be. 'My acts and desires,' wrote Teresa of herself in 1581, 'seem not to be as strong as they once were, for ... I have a desire much more powerful than any of them—that the will of God may be done.'[84] Except during brief intervals, she longed neither for death nor for life.

Such is the picture, necessarily brief and inadequate, but full of vigour and beauty, which Teresa gives us of the Life of Union—unsurpassed, save for the Beatific Vision of the life to come.

VIII

THE LAST JOURNEYS
(1577–1582)

IN July 1577, after spending a full year in Toledo, Teresa made a journey to Ávila to arrange for the transference of St. Joseph's from the jurisdiction of the Ordinary to that of the Carmelite Order. The helpfulness, at the time of its foundation, of the then Bishop, Don Álvaro de Mendoza, had made it advisable to place the convent under his obedience, and it remained so for fifteen years, when Don

---

[82] *Ibid.*
[83] I.C. VII, iii (II, 343).
[84] R. VI (I, 335).

Álvaro was translated to Palencia. This seemed a good moment for regularizing the position, and accordingly her confessor sent her to Ávila to discuss it with the new Bishop, and also with the nuns, whose agreement was essential. Both parties made objections, but eventually agreed, and the transference was made quite smoothly. None the less, Teresa remained at Ávila for nearly two years.

Her journey there interrupted the composition of the *Interior Castle*, which, as we saw, she had begun in June and was not to take up until October. It is not surprising that she should have been unable to do so sooner. That same June had seen the death of Ormaneto, and, with the arrival, in August, of his successor, Sega, began the 'great storm of trials'[1] for the Discalced Reform which ended, as Teresa had foreseen it must do when she first wrote to the King, in the division of the Calced and the Discalced into two Orders. But this was not to happen until 1580; and the intervening years were filled with incidents, often childish in nature, which show what a degree of tension the conflict had attained.

There were, for example, the extraordinary scenes at the Incarnation in October 1577, a few weeks before St. John of the Cross, who had remained there as confessor, was kidnapped and imprisoned in the prison-cell at Toledo.[2] Teresa's three years as Prioress there had been followed by three full years as Prioress of St. Joseph's, and many of the Incarnation nuns wanted her back again for three years more. She herself, no doubt, would have preferred greater freedom, for during most of the former triennium the condition of the convent had forced her to suspend her journeyings and reside there, whereas during the triennium at St. Joseph's she had been able to delegate much of her work and resume her *rôle* of Mother Foundress: she had, in

[1] R. XXXVII (I, 353). Cf. p. 123, above.
[2] *Spirit of Flame*, pp. 42–53.

fact, during those three years, made no less than four new foundations. So her non-election to the Incarnation for a second term can only have been a relief to her. What troubled her was the way in which it came about. 'These affairs of ours are just like a comedy,' she had written in one of her lighter moments.[3] 'Just like a tragedy,' she must more often have thought.

The election at the Incarnation was presided over by the Provincial of the Observance, who had evidently made up his mind that Teresa should be defeated. What took place she relates in one of her letters:

I must tell Your Reverence of something which has happened at the Incarnation, the like of which I do not believe has ever before been seen. On the order of Tostado,[4] the Provincial of the Calced came here a fortnight ago, to preside at the election, and he threatened any who gave their votes for me with severe censure and excommunication. But they took no notice of all that and fifty-five of them voted for me just as if he had said nothing to them at all. And as each of them handed her vote to the Provincial he excommunicated her and abused her, and pounded the voting-papers with his fist and struck them and burned them. This happened a fortnight ago, but he has left these nuns without Communion and forbidden them to hear Mass or enter the choir, even when the Divine Office is not being said. And nobody is allowed to speak to them, not even their confessors or their own parents. And the most amusing thing is that, on the day after this election by poundings, the Provincial summoned these nuns to a fresh election; to which they replied that there was no need to hold another since they had held one already. On hearing this, he excommunicated them again, and, summoning the remaining nuns, forty-four of them, he declared another prioress elected, and applied to Tostado to have this election confirmed.[5]

The confirmation was duly sent, but the majority who had elected St. Teresa were obdurate, declared that they would only obey the nominee of the minority as sub-prioress and sent Tostado a message of protest. He, however, showed equal intransigence and said that Teresa

---

[3] LL. 171 (February 27–28, 1577).
[4] Cf. p. 121, above.
[5] LL. 198, written in October 1577, to M. María de San José, Prioress of the Reformed House at Seville.

could go and live at the Incarnation if she liked, but was not to be its prioress. 'I don't know how it will end,' she sighs.[6] Apparently the nuns who had voted for her kept importuning her to take up the office to which they had elected her. 'I would willingly forgive them,' she says, 'if they would leave me in peace. I have no desire to be in that Babel, especially with my poor health, which gets worse when I live in that house. May God do as is most pleasing to Him and set me free from them.'[7]

Some weeks before all this St. Teresa had again written to the King[8] protesting against calumnies which she alleged to have been circulated about Gracián, and, in a postscript, against the activities of Tostado. By the beginning of November the postscript at least had borne fruit, and, though the nuns at the Incarnation were still holding out against their minority-prioress,[9] the Royal Council had censured Tosado, who thereupon left for Rome. So Teresa was able to start writing again, but, less than a week after the *Interior Castle* was finished, she was writing to the King once more, this time about the kidnapping of John and his companion from the Incarnation. Throughout her correspondence (our chief source for this period, about which the *Foundations* says nothing) we find continual allusions to the conflict:

> Of your charity commend it to God, for I don't believe we shall ever have done with these disturbances until we are a separate province.[10]
>
> I don't know where the absurd things these people are doing will stop. May God of His mercy put them right, as He sees the need.[11]
>
> Jesus be with my Father and deliver him from these Egyptians.

[6] LL. 198, to M. María de San José.
[7] *Ibid.*
[8] LL. 195 (September 18, 1577).
[9] LL. 199 (November 10, 1577). They were excommunicated in all for two months (LL. 205: December 7, 1577) and absolved only (LL. 207: December 10, 1577) at the request of the King.
[10] LL. 205 (December 7, 1577).
[11] LL. 207 (December 10, 1577).

I tell you, the things they have done to these poor nuns have horrified me.... They have all banded together against this Reform and I have heard too much of the uproar they are making.[12]

The less she was able to go and vist her nuns the more she would write to comfort them—and, adds a contemporary, 'it was always a great happiness to them when they saw her writing.'[13]

At about this time Teresa reinforced the effect of her letters to the King by travelling to the Escorial to see him,[14] probably on the burning theme of the activities of Tostado. 'Imagine,' she writes to a friend, in short, clipt sentences quite unlike her usual style, 'what this poor woman must have felt when she saw so great a King before her. I was terribly embarrassed. I began to address him; but, when I saw his penetrating gaze fixed on me—the kind of gaze that goes deep down to the very soul—it seemed to pierce me through and through; so I lowered my eyes and told him what I wanted as briefly as I could. When I had finished telling him about the matter I looked up at him again. His face seemed to have changed. His expression was gentler and more tranquil. He asked me if I wanted anything further. I answered that what I had asked for was a great deal. Then he said: "Go away in peace, for everything shall be arranged as you wish...." I knelt to thank him for his great favour. He bade me rise, and making this poor nun, his unworthy servant, the most charming bow I ever saw, held out his hand to me again, which I kissed. Then I went away full of jubilation.'[15]

The year 1577 ended badly for Teresa, for on the night of Christmas Eve she fell downstairs and broke her left arm. She appears to have climbed the stairs to the little chapel and been seized with giddiness at the top; but her

[12] LL. 219 (March 11, 1578).
[13] *Documents*, IV (III, 343).
[14] The date of the interview is uncertain, but is generally placed between December 11 and 17, 1577.
[15] LL. Appendix XI (*Obras*, ed. P. Silverio, IX, 266–7).

cousin, M. María de San Jerónimo, assures us that 'it must have been the devil who threw her down,' a view, so Ribera tells us, which was highly popular with her daughters. She herself, when asked to decide the question, proffered the cryptic remark that the devil 'would do much worse things than that, if he were allowed to.'[16] The sequel to the accident was what one might expect of those days. No one could be found to set the arm, the only available person, a *curandera* from Medina, being ill. Eventually she came, and the bone had to be broken again and re-set, and even this 'intolerably painful' operation was only partially successful. More than four months have passed when she writes to Gracián and reports progress:

> Oh, my Father, I was quite forgetting! The woman came to cure my arm. The Prioress of Medina did very well to send her, though it cost her no little trouble—and the treatment cost me no little either! I had lost the use of my wrist, and it hurt and tried me terribly, as it was so long since I fell. Still, I was happy at experiencing some tiny part of what was endured by Our Lord. I think I am cured, though it tortures me so much that I can't be sure if the cure is complete. I can move my hand easily, however, and raise my arm as far as my head; but it will be some time before I am quite well again.[17]

And now we must leave Teresa to her convalescence and take up the history of the Reform, since for a year or so more happenings that affect her will be taking place outside her convent than within it.

The persecution of the Reform was at its height. The Discalced were forbidden to receive any further novices or open new houses. Gracián was confined to the Discalced priory at Alcalá de Henares, where he was to live under discipline. St. John of the Cross was still in his Toledo prison. St. Teresa was ordered to remain at Ávila. It seemed, she wrote in a motherly letter to the Seville nuns ('Never have I loved you as I do now,' it begins), as if the Lord Jesus were asleep; but never fear, 'when the storm

---

[16] *Documents* IV (III, 344, n.).
[17] LL. 229 (May 7, 1578).

rises, He will still the winds,' and soon 'the sea will swallow up those who make war upon us as it did King Pharaoh.'[18]

Philip, fortunately, continued to interest himself in the Discalced. Finding it impossible to change Sega's mind and impracticable to override his orders, he worked through his four assessors, who took over all the documents in the case for examination, and also through the Royal Council, which insisted that the charges against Gracián should be heard. Of these he was cleared, and, after a little more than a year, allowed to leave Alcalá de Henares. Once freed, he set to work to obtain help from Rome. The project of sending two Discalced friars there was revived and two excellent men were chosen: Fray Diego de la Trinidad, Prior of the Pastrana house, and Fray Juan de Jesús, generally known (so common was the name) by his surname Roca, and, because of this patronymic and his determined temperament, nicknamed 'the Rock of Bronze.' Meanwhile, in April 1579, Sega, coming round a little, appointed a Visitor to the Reform, who was not only kindly disposed to it, but, being too unwell to travel to Andalusia, named Gracián as his deputy. Finally, Philip's assessors, having examined the whole matter, decided to recommend the longed-for partition of the Order, and in November 1579 Sega, apparently quite won over, forwarded the recommendation to Rome, endorsing it with his own approval.

It was not until the May of 1579, when the two friars, disguised as laymen, had set off for Rome, that Teresa was authorized to resume the visitation of her convents. At the end of June she left Ávila for a new period of great activity. Short stays sufficed at Medina, Valladolid and Alba de Tormes. At Salamanca, however, she remained for two and a half months. The house to which she had transferred her nuns six years earlier had not proved satisfactory and she had hoped to procure them a new one. In this she was

[18] LL. 264 (January 31, 1579).

disappointed. One of the saddest letters[19]—perhaps the first which makes us realize that age, ill-health and strain were beginning to tell on her—was written from here to Gracián. 'Oh, my Father,' she cries, 'what trials this house is costing me!' They had been kept out of it, of course, by the devil. These deceitful sons of Adam! The whole thing was settled: the owner himself had promised them the house and had signed the contract in the presence of witnesses, including his own lawyer. And then he had broken it—and not another house was to be found. And one grievance leads to another—the plight of the Salamancan sisters recalls the childish antics[20] of the nuns at Seville and their prioress, María de San José, who have 'the finest house in the place' and yet want to leave it for another. And there is something else. Teresa cannot 'quiet her suspicions'—and no wonder, for she is weak and full of worries. She has been ill-treated. By whom? Why, by Gracián himself. *He has not been writing to her often enough.* Pathetic old saint! Human old saint! She is lonely and craves friendship. 'Beg that gentleman,' she pleads, using the third person, perhaps a little shyly, perhaps half-playfully:

> Beg that gentleman, though he may be careless by nature, not to be so with her; for, where there is love, it cannot slumber so long.[21]

No house in Salamanca being obtainable, Teresa had to leave her nuns where they were, for a new house had been acquired at Malagón, and there she arrived, to see the community into it, at the end of November, remaining until February 1580. She was happy at Malagón. It was a peaceful backwater—the sort of place she had 'been desiring for many years ... and no one bothers any more

---

[19] LL. 290 (Octobre 4, 1579).
[20] *Rapacería.* I do not know why several English writers have translated the word as 'foxiness,' which conveys quite an inaccurate impression.
[21] LL. 290.

about Teresa de Jesús than if there were no such person in the world.'[22] Her health, too—perhaps for that very reason—had been better; and, though the convent had been suffering from inefficient government (she had narrowly escaped being made Prioress herself), and this gave her a good deal of work and anxious thought, she was not the woman to be afraid of either. The transference of the community to the new house, she relates, was 'an occasion of great rejoicing,' and the nuns were so happy that, as she delightfully puts it, 'they looked like nothing so much as lizards coming out into the sun in summer-time.'[23]

From Malagón she went on a journey southwards to Villanueva de la Jara, a small town just beyond the borders of La Mancha. Here she stayed for a month and made the thirteenth of her foundations, the first for over four years.

For quite as long as that it had been under consideration, for it was in 1576 that Teresa had received letters from the municipality and the parish priest of Villanueva, asking if she would make a foundation for a group of women who had for some years been living as a self-constituted religious community in a neighbouring hermitage. She was loth to do so: the town was too small to support them; they would be a long way from her other convents; and, though the reports of them were good, 'it would be very difficult for them to accustom themselves to our way of life now that they were used to their own.'[24] On her confessor's advice, however, she refrained from giving a direct negative, and the matter dragged on, through the years of persecution, until one day a message reached her at Malagón that the municipality would bind itself to provide for the foundation's bodily needs and the question was settled by a command from God in prayer. So she took two nuns from Malagón, called at Toledo on the way for two more, and, after making a second halt at La Roda,

[22] LL. 297 (December 1579).
[23] L. 295 (December 12, 1579).
[24] F. XXVIII (III, 152).

where her old friend Fray Antonio de Jesús was living just then, reached Villanueva on the eighth day after her departure.

It was a beautiful spring Sunday morning; and the reception given her by the people, following a series of boisterous welcomes at the villages on the road[25] must have sent Teresa's thoughts hurrying back twelve years and more to her stealthy arrival, at dead of night, in Medina, or even to the timorous nocturnal advance upon the house that was to be their convent at Seville, with every shadow looking like an inimical friar. Distance, no doubt, had lent enchantment to the prospect of a visit from the famous Mother Foundress. Long before they reached the town they could hear the bells ringing. Beside the first houses were waiting the entire town council, with the parish priest and various other notabilities, to escort them to the church, which was some way from the future convent. The procession entered the church; the organ pealed; the choir sang the Te Deum; and then, accompanied by the Blessed Sacrament and a statue of Our Lady, nuns, priests, councillors and people set out again for the new foundation. 'We,' recounts Teresa, 'in our white mantles and with veiled faces, walked in the middle of the procession immediately after the Most Holy Sacrament.'[26]

Along the route altars had been erected, at each of which a station was made, and it was some time before they arrived at their journey's end, where the sisters, overjoyed at the prospect of recognition after nearly six years of community life, were waiting to receive them. Teresa's description is the more pathetic for its simplicity:

> They were ... so thin that it was clear they had been living a life of great penitence.... Their sole fear was that, when the nuns saw the poverty and smallness of the house, they might go away again.[27]

[25] Ana de San Bartolomé.
[26] F. XXVIII (III, 162).
[27] F. XXVIII (III, 164).

They had done their best, poor things, to organize their life according to the ideals of a religious community, but there is gentle and even loving irony in Teresa's description of the limited success which they had with the recital of the Divine Offices.

> Only one of them read well and the remainder could only read a little, and their breviaries were not all of the same kind. Some of them were of the old Roman kind and had been given them by clergy who were no longer using them. Others they had got as they could. As they read so badly they would spend many hours on them. They did not recite the Office where anyone from outside could hear them. God will have accepted their intention and labour, but they can have said very little that was correct.[28]

But, for all her alertness to the humorous aspect of the situation, Teresa saw much in the lives of these earnest women that made her praise God. Their sharing of authority, their constancy in devotion, their attempts at self-direction by reading, even the 'orderly way' in which they organized their household tasks won from her a simple tribute of admiration. 'The more I had to do with them the more pleased I was I had come.'[29]

> The truth is that these nuns were so good that, however many difficulties and trials they might meet, they would bear them all with the help of the Lord, for they desire to suffer in His service; and any sister who does not feel this desire must not consider herself a true Discalced nun, for our desires must be directed, not towards rest but towards suffering, so that we may in some degree imitate our true Spouse. May it please His Majesty to give us grace for this. Amen.

In March 1580, Teresa was sent for from Villanueva to go north to Valladolid and discuss with the Bishop of Palencia—her old friend Don Álvaro de Mendoza of Ávila—the possibility of founding a Reformed convent in his cathedral city. We may think of this summons as beginning the last stage of Teresa's travail on earth. Both there and at Malagón, and on her recent journeys, she had been un-

28 F. XXVIII (III, 164).
29 F. XXVIII (III, 164-5).

usually well: 'not for many days,' she says, 'not, indeed, I believe, for years, had my health been so good.'[30] But she had been leading a dangerously active life for a woman of sixty-five who, over forty years earlier, had been given up for dead, and it was not surprising that, soon after reaching Toledo, she had a heart attack—'one of the worst attacks of paralysis and heart trouble that I have had in my life.' Yet so great was her vitality that, two days later, she was well enough to talk at the grille with Gracián's masterful rival, Doria,[31] who had come north from Seville. It is generally thought that she was attacked by the *catarro universal*, a kind of influenza, which swept Europe in 1580, and which would no doubt have affected her heart.

While she was making a halt in Segovia a very depressing letter came from her brother Lorenzo, saying that he was ailing and had forebodings' of an early death. She wrote at once to give him a sisterly scolding for 'thinking such foolish things and being oppressed by what won't happen.'[32] That letter he can barely have received. A week after it was written he had a sudden hæmorrhage of the lungs and died in a few hours.[33] So, instead of going straight on to Valladolid, where she was to have met her revered Don Álvaro, Teresa turned aside and went back to his home in Ávila, to look over his papers and arrange his affairs for his children, one of whom, Teresita de Jesús, though only fourteen, was a nun of Reformed Carmel. Then she went on, by way of Medina del Campo, to Valladolid, arriving there on August 8, nearly five months after leaving Villanueva de la Jara.

Here she had a recurrence of the illness which had attacked her at Toledo. It was 'so serious that they thought I should die.'[34] Perhaps the condition of her heart had

---

[30] LL. 314 (April 3, 1580).
[31] *Spirit of Flame*, pp. 77–8.
[32] LL. 325 (June 19, 1580).
[33] LL. 326, 342 (July 4, 1580, December 28, 1580).
[34] F. XXIX (III, 166). Cf. LL. 336 (October 25, 1580): 'They did not think I should live.'

been aggravated by her anxieties and sorrows. During the past few months she had lost, not only her brother, but several other close friends. In spite of the way she had rallied Lorenzo, she began to feel that her time might be short too. One of these attacks would surely carry her off. 'We ought to exercise our minds on how to die rather than on how to live,' she wrote from Segovia to M. María. 'I am four years older than he (Lorenzo) was and yet I never quite manage to die (*no me acabo de morir*). Please God,' she adds, 'that my staying here may be to do Him some service.'[35]

The illness left her with a quite unwonted lassitude. Before going to Valladolid, she had been anxious to make the Palencia foundation, but now she felt that it was more than she could undertake. Why was this? She thought she would consult her 'great friend,' the Jesuit Ripalda. Was this disinclination to do anything due to physical weakness, she asked him, or was it the work of the devil? Neither, calmly replied Ripalda, who was clearly a first-rate psychologist. It was just 'cowardice—the effect of old age.'![36]

He could hardly have said anything which would have galvanized Teresa more quickly into action. She might be sixty-five, but she was not an old woman yet. 'I was quite sure this was not so,' she records, and 'he cannot have thought it was so, but said it to reprove me.' Immediately a foundation at Palencia became a practical proposition, and a foundation at Burgos, which had also been long mooted, too. 'I was now a great deal better.'[37]

So, on December 28, 1580, she left for Palencia, which is only thirty miles from Valladolid, and made the foundation on the next day. A furnished house, with 'beds and comforts in great abundance,' had been lent her for the first six months, and, with a return to her old and once well-founded desire for secrecy ('I saw it would be safer if

[35] LL. 326 (July 4, 1580).
[36] F. XXIX (III, 167).
[37] *Ibid.*

no one knew'), they moved in—five nuns and a lay sister.
By the following June they had purchased a house of their
own and settled down in the happiest possible way:

> I should be sorry to be backward in praising all the kindness
> which I found in Palencia, both in the people as a whole and in
> individuals. It really seemed to me like the primitive Church, and
> it is not very common in the world today. They knew we had no
> money, and that they would have to feed us, yet not only did
> they not forbid us to settle among them but they said God was
> granting them the very greatest of favours.... May He be blessed
> for ever. Amen.[38]

It was during Teresa's stay at Palencia, at the Chapter
of Alcalá de Henares held on March 3, 1581, that Gracián
was elected Provincial of the Discalced Reform. The conflict within the Carmelite Order had been ended by its
partition. Teresa had always held that this was the only
solution of the problem; and it 'was all we desired for our
peace and quietness.'[39] Upon the division of the Order
Gracián at once became Vicar-General of the Discalced
Province, but at the Alcalá election his candidature for the
provincialate met with considerable opposition. Against
him were his youth—he was thirty-five—his alleged ame-
nability to flattery and the fact that he had held some
kind of office almost continuously since he entered the
Order. In his favour were his outstanding talent, energy
and enthusiasm and his close connection with the Mother
Foundress. In the issue, he was elected by a majority of
only one. It was not a happy beginning for the new
Province.

But, however small the majority, Teresa was delighted
at the result, and some of the letters are still extant which
she wrote him, on an emphatic, sometimes almost a peremptory note, giving him her views on the constitutions
and the government of the new province.[40] Before long

[38] F. XXIX (III, 174–5).
[39] F. XXIX (III, 175).
[40] LL. 350–2, 358 (February 1581).

she was writing him a very different kind of letter. Her
next foundation was to be at Soria, a town of some importance, but far distant from any of the other Reformed
houses, near the borders of Castile and Navarre. Which-
ever route she took, it would not be less than a hundred
and fifty miles from Palencia and she had believed that
Gracián would accompany her. She had been 'looking forward to the journey'—'I believe I should have been sorry
when it was over.' And then she hears from him that he
has decided instead to go to Valladolid, where a college for
the Reform was to be founded, and had arranged for her
companion to be the highly practical but not too sympathetic Fray Nicolás Doria. And Teresa, for once, was both
disappointed and hurt—and said so.

> I must confess to you, my Father, that the flesh is weak, and it
> has felt this more than I should have wished—a great deal, in fact.
> At least Your Paternity's departure might have been postponed
> till you could leave us in our new house, for a week sooner or
> later would not have mattered much. It has been terribly lonely
> here. . . .
>   Nothing will be right now, for, after all, the soul feels being
> away from the one who governs and soothes it. May God be
> served by all this![41]

It may not be fanciful to see in these pathetic lines an
indication of the Saint's growing physical weakness. Old—
yes, Ripalda was right—and worn out by two successive
illnesses, she might well dread this long and trying journey
without the companion who could best have given her
spiritual solace as well as practical help. At the last
moment the start was made rather quickly, several days
before the move of the Palencia nuns to their new house.
And Teresa's apprehensions proved excessive. 'The weather
helped us; the days' drives were not long; and so we had
little trouble on the way and enjoyed the journey.'[42] What
she particularly loved was the long stretch of road which
ran alongside the river Duero, for she never lost her love

[41] LL. 366 (May 24, 1581).
[42] F. XXX (III, 180).

of water—'it was a real refreshment to me, for the road was flat and often had river views *which were quite companionable.*'[43]

Their longest halt was made at Burgo de Osma, a small cathedral city whose Bishop, Teresa's old friend, Dr. Velázquez, had strongly supported the project for a Soria foundation. So popular was he that no sooner had they entered the diocese than the bare mention of his name procured them good lodgings. In the city, being himself ailing, he sent an envoy who took every care of them, and, when they left, 'the saintly Bishop was at one of the windows of his house and from it gave us his blessing.'[44]

From Palencia, Teresa had also written to the Bishop, giving him an account of her spiritual life, in one of the most precious documents that have come down to us from her.[45] The storms of these last years, we are glad to learn, are passing over her and leaving her true self unscathed. It 'feels as if the sufferings were wounding only its garments.'[46] Her soul remains in a state of 'quiet and calm,'[47] and she is content to await the fruition of God. Till the moment of her departure comes, she has no desire other than scope for increased service:

> All I want is to serve, even if service means great suffering, and sometimes I think that if I were to serve God from now until the end of the world it would be a small thing by comparison with the title of possession He has given me.[48]

With that aim always in view, she takes greater care than she used to do of her health, offering God that care as a sacrifice. She is still guided by voices and visions, and the visions are of the highest kind. At times she is depressed by her growing physical weakness, though she has no longer,

---

[43] LL. 378 (September 9, 1581): *que me hacía hasta compañía.* Italics mine.
[44] F. XXX (III, 180).
[45] Cf. p. 60, above.
[46] R. VI (I, 334).
[47] *Ibid.*
[48] *Ibid.*

as she had formerly, any 'disquiet and distress.'[49] Except when 'seriously oppressed by ill-health,' she has an almost continuous realization of the presence within her of the Blessed Trinity. Her 'one attachment is to the love of God'; never for a moment does her will swerve from His. 'My soul,' she ends,

> desires neither death nor life save for short periods when it longs to see God. But then its realization of the presence of these three Persons becomes so vivid as to afford relief to the distress caused by its absence from God and sustains the desire to live, if such be His will, in order that it may serve Him better. If through my intercession I could do anything to make a single soul love and praise Him more, and that only for a short time, it seems to me of greater moment than my being in glory.[50]

Not for long could Teresa remain in so distant an out-post as Soria. After two months, 'in the terrible heat' of a Castilian August, she made her way back to Ávila—a longer and more exacting journey than from Palencia to Soria, 'by a road which was very bad for carriages,' through Osma and Segovia and along the Sierra de Gua-darrama. Fray Nicolás had stayed only long enough to see the foundation deeds signed, and the companion who took his place, though very 'careful,' was somewhat weak in his topography, with results that give Teresa admirable scope for her powers of description. He could find his way as far as Segovia, but not by the carriage road. He

> took us up a road so bad that we often had to alight, and the carriage went over steep precipices till it almost hung in the air.[51]

If they chartered guides, 'they would take us as far as they knew the road to be good, and before we came to a bad part'—how like the calm and casual Spaniard even of the twentieth century!—'they would leave us and say they had now some business to do elsewhere.'

[49] R. VI (I, 335).
[50] R. VI (I, 335–7).
[51] F. XXX (III, 183).

Before reaching an inn... we had to endure a great deal of sun and often to risk the overturning of the carriage.... Although they would tell us that we were on the right road, we had often to retrace our steps.... I praise the Lord, Who was pleased to bring us safely out of that journey.[52]

At Segovia, Teresa was able to stay for a week in her own convent, where the nuns had been in great anxiety over her delay; she then went on to Ávila, arriving on September 5, and five days later being re-elected Prioress. But again she is sad. 'I am suffering very much from loneliness,' she writes, on the day before the election, 'and from the want of anyone to comfort me.'[53] What, lonely in her native Ávila, her home for over half a century? Yes, for her brother and many of her friends were no longer there— even at Soria the prospect of returning had oppressed her.[54] 'God help me,' she sighs, 'for the farther in this life I go, the fewer are the sources of comfort that I find there.'[55] And God was indeed helping her. Beside her Relation addressed to the Bishop of Osma may be placed a letter to María de San José, which gives another glimpse into her interior life. She is to read to P. Rodrigo Álvarez the last chapter of the *Interior Castle* and tell him that 'that person'—Teresa herself— 'has reached that Mansion, and attained the peace that goes with it, and so finds herself living a very restful life, and very learned men tell her that she is making good progress.'[56]

It was with a heavy heart, none the less, that she submitted once again to being elected superior. 'If the need for me is not great, it will be a vast relief not to have to stay there as prioress. I am really not fit for the task; it is beyond my strength.'[57] By the end of the year, as she picturesquely, if rather confusedly, put it, 'a hurly-burly

---

[52] *Ibid.*
[53] LL. 378 (September 9, 1581).
[54] LL. 375 (July 14, 1581).
[55] LL. 378 (September 9, 1581).
[56] LL. 385 (November 8, 1581).
[57] LL. 375 (July 14, 1581).

(*baraúnda*) of letters and business matters' was 'raining down on her.'[58] But less than a week later she left Ávila again, on a new series of journeyings—never, as it proved, to return to the grey old city.

The story of those last months need not be told in any detail. It is chiefly of journeys begun with great apprehensiveness, and punctuated by illnesses and fights against depression. First, in January 1582, to Medina, Valladolid (detained four days by illness), Palencia ('I am still pretty wretched'—*algo ruin*),[59] and Burgos, for her seventeenth foundation—the last.[60] How she survived that journey we may well wonder. January is at best a bitter month on the plateau ('it was so cold and the cold always affects me'),[61] and this January chanced to be a month of snow and rain. 'The roads were frequently flooded;' and Gracián, who accompanied the party of eight nuns, had to go on ahead of it to find passable tracks 'and help drag the carriages out of the marshes.'[62] It was quite usual for them to sink into the mud, when 'it would be necessary to take the animals from one carriage to drag out another.' Nor did it help matters to have 'drivers who were young and rather careless.' One episode of that nightmare-journey Teresa describes in detail. Near Burgos was a ford known locally as the Pontoons.

> Here, in many places, the water had risen so high that it had submerged these pontoons to such an extent that they could not be seen; and we could not find any way of going on, for there was water everywhere, and on both sides it was very deep. In fact, it is very rash of anyone to go that way, especially with carriages, for, if they heeled slightly, all would be lost.[63]

Not knowing what to do, they hired a guide who lived there and 'knew the best way through, but it was certainly

[58] LL. 400 (December 28, 1581).
[59] LL. 404 (January 16, 1582).
[60] The sixteenth had been made on January 20, at Granada, in her absence.
[61] F. XXXI (III, 188).
[62] F. XXXI (III, 190).
[63] *Ibid.*

a very dangerous one.' Before long, to use her own vivid phrase, Teresa saw that they were entering a 'world of water.' There was 'no sign of a path or a boat,' and, she adds, 'even I was not without fear, despite all the strength Our Lord had given me. What then must my companions have been?'[64]

Eventually they won through; and only at this point does the Saint remember to add that she was suffering all the time from a sore throat and a high temperature, which, as she puts it, surely in fun,

> prevented me from enjoying the incidents of the journey as much as I might.[65]

It is of this journey that the famous story is told of Teresa's complaint to Our Lord, of His reply: 'But that is how I treat My friends,' and of her ready retort: 'Yes, my Lord, and that is why Thou hast so few of them.' Authentic or not it may be, but it is highly characteristic.

At Burgos, where the devil had been more than usually active, a long time passed before the foundation could be made, and Teresa remained there for six months, partly occupying her time by completing the *Foundations*. No longer does she attempt to maintain any illusions about the state of her health: Ripalda might say what he liked now —her own words betray her: 'I was so old and ill.'

Old and ill, then, Teresa set out upon the journey which was to be her last. With her were two very dear companions—Teresita, Lorenzo's daughter, now a girl of sixteen, and Ana de San Bartolomé, a lay sister of about thirty, who constantly accompanied her, nursed her, saw to her comfort and was with her when she died. Ana, who subsequently became a choir-nun and took part in making foundations of the Reform outside Spain, has left an

---

[64] *Ibid.*

[65] F. XXXI (III, 191, where another interpretation is suggested). An account of this journey is given also by Ana de San Bartolomé (*Documents*, V: III, 355).

account of the Saint's last days which is the main source of the paragraphs that follow.

The goal of that last journey, never reached, was of course Ávila, for six months had elapsed since the Prioress of St. Joseph's had seen her convent. On her way she visited the convents at Palencia, Valladolid and Medina del Campo. At Valladolid, where she was detained by a fresh illness for nearly a month, a great disappointment awaited her. She had expected to find her beloved Gracián, but he had gone south, and she wrote to him almost bitterly:

> Your writing frequently is not enough to quench my grief....
> Your reasons for deciding to go did not seem to me sufficient....
> I have felt your absence so keenly that I have lost all desire to
> write to you.[66]

Though Teresa had left Burgos on July 26, it was only on September 16 that she reached Medina.

The last stage of the journey would have been a simple one, with which she was well acquainted. But unfortunately at Medina she was awaited by her old friend Fray Antonio de Jesús, whose life is so strangely intertwined both with her own last days and with those of St. John of the Cross. Antonio was now Vicar-Provincial, and, when she arrived, he told her that she was to turn off the main road and take the cross-country journey to Alba de Tormes in order to pay a visit to the Duchess of Alba, whose daughter-in-law was expecting a child and had asked that the 'saint' (as people so often called her now) might be allowed to come and give her her blessing.

Unfit though she was for further travelling, and longing to reach her desired haven, Teresa silently obeyed. But 'never,' declares Ana, 'had I seen her so sad about anything which her superiors had ordered her to do as about this.'[67] They left in a carriage quite unequal to the hilly roads,

[66] LL. 434 (September 1, 1582).
[67] *Documents*, V (III, 360).

and, when they came to a village near Peñaranda, the last place of any size on the journey, Teresa 'was so weak and in such pain that she fainted.' 'It made us all dreadfully sorry to see her like that,' continues Ana in her homely way, 'and we had nothing to give her but a few figs, which had to last her the night, for in the whole village we could not find so much as an egg.'[68]

> I was in anguish at seeing her in such straits and being unable to help her, but she comforted me and told me not to be grieved— the figs were extremely good and there were many poor people who would have less.[69]

On the next day, after a fruitless visit to another village in search of relief, they went on, and reached Alba de Tormes on September 20. The poor traveller was worn out —'so ill that she was unable to talk to the nuns'—and the child at whose birth she had come to be present had already arrived. 'Thank God,' she exclaimed when she heard this, 'there will be no need for this saint now!'

Once more that magnificent constitution, which had so often enabled her to rally after being thought at death's door, prevailed, and for a short time she got up and went about her religious duties. But soon she had to take to her bed again, and on the third day of her illness she asked to be given the Blessed Sacrament. Its very arrival brought strength to her. 'She sat up in bed,' related Ana, 'in such a spirited way that it looked as if she were going to get up; so they had to restrain her.' Her mind was clear and she knew that she would make only one more journey. She had no apprehensions now.

'My Lord,' she exclaimed—'with great joy'—'it is time to set out; may the journey be a propitious one and may Thy will be done.'

Her daughters came round her bedside and begged her for some words which should be of help to them in years

[68] *Ibid.*
[69] *Documents,* V (III, 360–1).

to come. But, practical to the last, she would only charge them always to keep strictly to their Rule and Constitutions. After that she said little more, except for 'repeating again and again' a verse from the Psalms of David:

> A sacrifice to God is an afflicted spirit: a contrite and humbled heart, O God, Thou wilt not despise.[70]

'On Saint Francis' Day,' ends Ana, 'at nine o'clock in the evening, Our Lord took her.'

She had fought a good fight; she had finished her course; she had kept the faith. 'I do not know,' she once wrote, 'how we can grieve for those who go to the land of safety.'[71]

[70] Ps. l. 19 (Douay Version).
[71] LL. 31 (November 7, 1571).

—————————————

IX

TERESA THE WRITER

'I NEVER knew, or saw, Mother Teresa while she lived on earth,' wrote Luis de León in his edition of the Saint's writings; 'but now that she lives in Heaven I do know her, and I see her almost continuously in two living images of herself which she left us—her daughters and her books.'[1]

We today are less fortunate than Fray Luis; for those great-hearted and steel-willed women who move across the stage of her times are known to too few of us even by name, and the chief source of our knowledge is her own letters. But the image of herself which she left in her books is as bright and as fresh as ever and she has probably more readers now than at any time in the past and certainly many times more than during her own life. P. Silverio estimates that 'no other book by a Spanish author is as widely known in Spain' as her *Life* or *Interior Castle*, 'with the single exception of Cervantes' immortal *Don Quixote*.'[2] In our own country the translations of Malone, Tobias Mathew and Abraham Woodhead made her popular in the seventeenth century and two hundred years later a revival of that interest was started by Dalton and Lewis and fostered more recently by the admirable versions of the Benedictine nuns of Stanbrook Abbey and the

---

[1] The entire letter is reproduced in C.W. III 368–78 (*Documents*, VII).
[2] C.W. I, xxxviii.

scholarly works of the Carmelite Father Zimmerman. Those best able to judge are aware that in the past decade this interest has risen to new heights, for, during the period of bitter trial from which we have lately emerged, many have found in St. Teresa and St. John of the Cross the iron tonic they most needed.

Essentially, the appeal of St. Teresa is attributable to the power of her teaching and of her sanctified life, which has influenced people of all kinds, often in the most unusual circumstances. So much those who have read her books— and perhaps even those whose knowledge of her has been gained through this little book—would expect. The surprising fact is that a woman who was no scholar, and who wrote much as she spoke, to be read only by the few, should have won such a reputation as a writer, and become one of the classics both of the literature of Spain and of the world-wide literature of Christian devotion. It seems right, then, that in taking leave of her we should cast a backward glance, first at Teresa the writer and then at Teresa the saint.

As a writer, she has the rare gift of appealing both to the most learned readers, as a natural stylist of rare merit, and to the least learned—to the man in the street, and still more to the woman in the kitchen—as intensely human, as one just like themselves. 'For the love of God,' she cried, when asked for a new book, 'let me work at my spinning-wheel. . . . I am not meant to write: I have neither the health nor the intelligence for it.'[3] There spoke the woman in the kitchen. None the less, she put aside her spinning and complied with the demand. And the result was—the *Interior Castle*!

Every woman in the kitchen feels a kinship with her, for she says exactly what they themselves would say if a book were demanded of them. She has so much housework and so little leisure:

[3] C.W. I, xxxix.

I am almost stealing the time for writing, and that with great difficulty, for ... I am living in a poor house and have numerous things to do.[4]

Her memory is bad:

I only wish I could write with both hands, so as not to forget one thing while I am saying another.[5]

As I have a poor memory, I expect many very important things will be omitted, and others will be put in which might well be left out: just as might be expected, in fact, of one with my witlessness and stupidity.[6]

She is always afraid of repeating herself or of losing the thread of her writing—and apparently it never occurred to her that the best way to avoid this would be to reread her preceding pages:

It is a long time since I wrote the last chapter and I have had no chance of returning to my writing, so that, without reading through what I have written, I cannot remember what I said. However ... it will be best if I go right on without troubling about the connection.[7]

And, worst of all, especially in that troublesome book about her foundations, there are those dreadful dates, which she never *can* call to mind:

All this lasted more than a month, as far as I remember, but I have a bad memory for dates and so I might be wrong.[8]

However, her readers must not take it too tragically: 'You must always understand my dates to be approximate —they are of no great importance.'[9] And one chapter which has been bothering her a good deal she rounds off quite happily:

In giving the years in which these foundations have been made I have some suspicion that I may be making mistakes, although I have made every effort to recall the exact dates. This is not of

---

4 L. X (I, 61).
5 W.P. XX, (E) (II, 88).
6 F. Prologue (III, xxiii).
7 W.P. XIX (II, 76).
8 F. XXV (III, 132).
9 *Ibid.*

great importance, for corrections can be made later, and I am speaking as well as my memory will allow me to do, so if there should be some errors it will not make much difference.[10]

Which of us that is scared at the idea of writing a book, or which of us that remembers how difficult it was to write one when he first tried, would not have a warm corner in his heart for the woman who wrote all that? And that is why Teresa, the writer with the 'sweet disorder' in her literary dress, with her errors, her digressions, her disconnected remarks, her ellipses, her irrelevant asides—yes, and her spelling mistakes!—captivates the ordinary person at the first attack. She is the ordinary person's ideal author, and the not very skilful author's patron saint.

That is why, purely from the literary standpoint, she is at her best in that incomparable collection of letters which, by the greatest good fortune, has come down to us in such abundance. There are nearly five hundred of them and fresh ones are being found continually. Even while P. Silverio's great three-volume edition was passing through the press, over twenty years ago, another handful came to light and had to be included in an appendix. Some day, in two final volumes of the *Complete Works,* I hope to translate the entire collection, but I feel so sure that Spain's recent years of convulsion will have thrown up more discoveries that I have postponed doing this for the present.

The great advantage, to Teresa, of the letter over the autobiography and the treatise was that in it none of her defects as a writer—her shocking memory, her lack of leisure, her tendency to digress, her uncertainty about dates—was of the least importance. No one noticed them. In fact, she forgot about them herself. And the result is a simply magnificent canvas portraying the Mother Foundress, surrounded by almost the whole of the people who enter into her life-story: the beloved Gracián, María de San José, the gifted Sevilian prioress, the serene Ana de Jesús, the sinister Doria, the generous brother Lorenzo, his

[10] F. XX (III, 103).

little daughter Teresita, Don Alonso Velázquez, the good Bishop of Osma, and a whole gallery more. And in illumining these, Teresa unconsciously throws the stronger light of all upon herself. A vast amount of the detail in the letters is of the most trivial nature—there are an amazing number of references to all kinds of food. A great deal more confirms the impression given by her major works of her extraordinary aptness for all kinds of business. From the letters, too, we can realize better than from any of her other writings what a trial her continual ill-health was to her, and for those who would share in imagination the trials of her journeyings the letters form an indispensable complement to the *Foundations*.

But their great contribution to our knowledge of St. Teresa is one which there is not space to develop here: they tell us so much of her relations with other people. In them, as nowhere else, we learn how much she prized the wisdom and revered the sanctity of St. John of the Cross. In them we have first-hand material for a study of the peculiar bond which united her to Gracián. We can see the conflict between the Observance and the Reform as she saw it. We can judge from her letters to her little communities how she would speak to them, and deal with them, on her visits. We can penetrate deeply into her relations with her superiors, and from the discussions which she carries on with her collaborators learn much of their characters and of her own. And all this against a background which is completely natural. She makes no attempt to hide either her elation or her despondency. There would be something almost profane in the unveiling of that saintly yet human personality were it not that, in her major works, she herself opens it to us freely. On all these grounds a close study of the letters of St. Teresa is to be warmly commended: I know none more fascinating in the literature of sixteenth-century Spain.

A second collection very easy to overlook is that little crop of verses, dignified with the title of 'poems'—a title

their author would certainly have disclaimed for them—
which I have translated at the end of the third volume of
the *Complete Works*. She herself had no illusions about
their literary worth: in the *Life* she describes herself as 'a
person who, though no poet, composed some verses, in a
very short time, which were full of feeling.'[11] She was
wrong in thinking herself no poet: the *Interior Castle* and
the *Exclamations*, her treatment of such similitudes as the
garden, the silkworm, the garrison, the palace made of a
diamond prove that. But almost invariably her poetry
expresses itself, not in verse, but in prose. Just once or
twice, inspired by Divine love and remembering some of
the glowing lines of the secular *cancioneros*, or song-books,
of her time, which she must have read in her young days as
assiduously as chivalric novels, she did write verse which
was true poetry. For the first of her poems I have found
two possible sources in the song-books and both in artistry
and in the sublimity of her theme she outstrips each:

> *O Loveliness, that dost exceed*
> *All other loveliness we know,*
> *Thou woundest not, yet pain'st indeed,*
> *And painlessly the soul is freed*
> *From love of creatures here below.*

> *O wondrous juncture, that dost bind*
> *Two things that nature parts in twain,*
> *I know not why thou com'st untwin'd,*
> *Since thou canst strengthen mortal mind*
> *And make it count its ills as gain.*

> *Things being-less thou dost unite*
> *With Being that can know no end.*
> *Thou endest not, yet endest quite;*
> *Unforc'd to love, Thou lov'st at sight:*
> *Thy nothingness Thou dost transcend.*[12]

[11] L. XVI (I, 97–8).
[12] *Poems*, VI (III, 283–4; cf. n. 2).

But, with this and occasional other exceptions, it is solely for their human appeal that we read Teresa's verses. Charming, for example, are her simple carols, with their anachronistic theology, featuring conventionalized shepherds who are suspiciously suggestive of the contemporary pastoral romances. Moving are the artless hymns—call them doggerel, if you like: Teresa would have agreed with you—of which the spirit, suffused as it is with eloquence, more than atones for the deficiencies of the letter:

> *Thine I am; for Thou didst make me;*
> *Thine, for Thou alone didst save me;*
> *Thine—Thou couldst endure to have me;*
> *For Thine own didst deign to take me;*
> *Never once didst Thou forsake me.*
> *Ruined were I but for Thee:*
> *What wilt Thou have done with me? ...*[13]

And here must not be forgotten those rough, unrhymed lines found after her death in a breviary which, writes Gracián, 'she was using for her prayers when Our Lord called her to Heaven from Alba.' They are generally known in English as 'St. Teresa's Book-mark.'

> *Let nothing disturb thee;*
> *Let nothing dismay thee;*
> *All things pass:*
> *God never changes.*
> *Patience attains*
> *All that it strives for.*
> *He who has God*
> *Finds he lacks nothing:*
> *God alone suffices.*[14]

But I confess to a personal weakness for some of the really dreadful verses which the Mother Foundress wrote

[13] *Poems,* II (III, 279).
[14] *Poems,* IX (III, 288).

for her communities—verses with strongly marked rhymes or assonances, jog-trotting along with a cheery rhythm which those unlettered nuns no doubt thought absolutely delightful. They would probably join in the refrains:

> *Let us be most mortified,*
> *Humble, though the world deride,*
> *Setting happiness aside,*
> Nuns of Carmel.

> *Let us, as we vow'd, obey,*
> *Never from obedience stray,*
> *For it is our aim and stay,*
> Nuns of Carmel....[15]

So well did she (and they) like this that she repeated the performance, this time putting in an extra line, and an extra rhyme, for good measure:

> *Let us take our cross each day,*
> *Follow Jesus as we may;*
> *Him our Light and Him our Way*
> *Let us follow, glad and gay,*
> Nuns of Carmel.

> *Your profession-vows are three:*
> *Guard them all most jealously.*
> *They will keep you ever free*
> *From sadness and despondency,*
> Nuns of Carmel....[16]

Some of these verses—such, probably, as the dialogue-fragment:

> *'Maiden, who brought thee here*
> *Out of the valley of woe?'*
> *'God and good fortune did so'*[17]

[15] *Poems,* X (III, 289).
[16] *Poems,* XX (III, 299–300).
[17] *Poems,* XXIV (III, 304).

were written for the professions of Discalced nuns. And
beneath the wooden language and unskilful rhyming, faith-
fully reproduced in these versions, we can glimpse the
simple dignity of the ceremony in some 'little Bethlehem':

> *My sister, you are giv'n this veil*
> *In token that your watch you take,*
> *And your reward in Heaven's at stake;*
> So you must watch and never fail.
>
> *This comely veil that you will wear*
> *Reminds you of your Lord's command.*
> *On sentry-duty you must stand*
> *Until at last your Spouse draw near*
> *And unexpectedly appear*
> *Like to the robber in the tale;*
> So you must watch and never fail. . . .[18]

At its close, all the nuns would join in a hymn of praise,
composed specially for the occasion by this wonderful
Mother of theirs, who could do almost anything:

> *Since while still in prison*
>   *We to God are dear,*
> Sing we the religion
>   Which we practise here.
>
> *O what feasts supernal*
>   *Jesus makes today;*
> *With His love eternal*
>   *Lights us on our way.*
> *As the Cross we follow*
>   *We will never fear:*
> Sing we the religion
>   Which we practise here. . . .[19]

But there came one sad day when the rough frieze habits
of the nuns of St. Joseph's were found to be infested with

[18] *Poems*, XXV (III, 304).
[19] *Poems*, XXX (III, 310).

what it was common to describe euphemistically as 'bad people'—*mala gente*—or, as we should say, 'nasty creatures.' Of the precise steps which St. Teresa took to cleanse them, or to provide others, we are ignorant, but, knowing her, we may be sure they were efficient ones. However, after the process was completed, to make assurance doubly sure, she organized a little procession, singing a prophylactic hymn in the last two lines of which her daughters would obediently join:

St. Teresa:

> *Daughters, you've the Cross upon you,*
> > *Have courage too.*
> *Since salvation He has won you,*
> > *He'll bring you through.*
> *He'll direct you, He'll defend you,*
> > *If Him you please:*

All:

> Do Thou keep all nasty creatures
> > Out of this frieze.

St. Teresa:

> *Drive away whate'er molests you*
> > *With fervent prayer;*
> *Nothing else so surely tests you*
> > *If love is there.*
> *God will help you if within you*
> > *Firm trust He sees:*

All:

> Do Thou keep all nasty creatures
> > Out of this frieze.

St. Teresa:

> *Since you came prepared to die here*
> > *Be not dismay'd.*
> *Ne'er must things that creep and fly here*
> > *Make you afraid.*
> *Help your God will always send you*
> > *'Gainst plagues like these:*

ALL:

> Do Thou keep all nasty creatures
> Out of this frieze.[20]

Yes, for their background and atmosphere we could as little spare these thirty-one songs and hymns as a like number of pages of the *Foundations*.

But why has St. Teresa won such fame with the stylists? Why, notwithstanding her lack of learning, is she accepted as one of the greatest writers of prose in the Spanish language? What are the characteristic qualities of her writing?

The answer to each of those questions is the same that we shall give to every such question that can be asked about her, whether as a writer or as a saint. *She was just herself.*

That, in the first place, is why, on occasion, she can be surprisingly difficult. She might be expected to be easier to read than St. John of the Cross: actually, she is often much harder. For, lofty and sometimes impossible of comprehension as is his theme, his expression of it is as clear as crystal and his orderly mind makes him deceptively easy to follow. St. Teresa, on the other hand, even in dealing with every-day matters, writes with the force of an impetuous torrent: ideas and phrases tumble about in her mind and come out in almost any order. It is a testimony to her natural gifts that the general sense of what she writes is hardly ever in doubt, but the precise force of a word, a phrase or a clause is often very hard to determine. It may be of interest to set on record that, though I have often consulted Spanish scholars upon the exact meaning of some doubtful phrase, more illuminating replies have as a rule been obtained from simple, unlettered people in Teresa's own Ávila or in two other Castilian cities which I happen to know well—Valladolid and Burgos.

[20] *Poems*, XXXI (III, 311–12).

But her obscurity is as frequently due to the virility of her language as to its abundance. Never, even when her ideas are flowing most freely, is she merely wordy; and at her best she practises word-economy in a very high degree. Nothing could be terser or more vigorous than:

> 'Rest, indeed!' I would say. 'I need no rest; what I need is crosses.'[21]
> Either you believe this or you do not: if you do, why do you wear yourselves to death with worry?[22]
> If Thou wilt (send me) trials, give me strength and let them come.[23]

or than the admirable conciseness of the 'Book-mark.'

Now again and again this style can be effectively rendered into our own language, which yields nothing to any other in its genius for conciseness and vigour. It is a great pity that past translators should so often have been content with weak paraphrases. But from time to time her terseness becomes so telegraphic that expansion is essential, and yet, in the Spanish, the meaning remains perfectly clear. In the *Life*, for instance, speaking admiringly of theologians who are members of religious Orders, she commends their plain living and high thinking. 'And then,' she goes on, 'think of the scant sleep they get: nothing but trials, nothing but crosses!' That is as economical expression as can be given to the ideas in English, but the Spanish, though no less perspicuous, is barely half the length:

> With this, bad sleep, all trial, all cross![24]

Or, in the *Foundations*, speaking of nuns afflicted with melancholia, she surmises, as we might of the modern child, that their rebelliousness could often be checked by a little more discipline. Or at least, she says, 'I know it is so in some; for, when they have been brought before a person

[21] L. XIII (I, 76).
[22] W.P. XXIX (II, 120).
[23] W.P. XXXII (II, 138).
[24] L. XIII (I, 82).

they are afraid of, I have seen them become docile, so I know they can if they like.' Those thirty-four words are represented by only nineteen in the Spanish, a literal translation of which would read:

> I mean in some, for I have seen that, when there is whom to fear, they become docile and can.[25]

Terseness, virility and vigour, then, are among the qualities which Teresa infused into the Spanish language. Closely connected with them is the purity of her speech. She was far from being the only one, or even the first, of the Spanish mystics to write in the vernacular, but the Spanish of many of her contemporaries—like the eloquent Luis de Granada—is highly involved and smacks very strongly of Latin. Teresa was no Latinist: 'God preserve my daughters from priding themselves on their Latin,' she had exclaimed once when the cultured María de San José had used some Latin phrase in a letter.[26] Her vocabulary was that of the people: any word in common use was good enough for her, while any word that was not, apart from a few technical terms, was at once suspect. When she quotes Latin, her spelling, like much of her Spanish spelling, is so phonetic as to be hardly recognizable. Like all good Castilian writers, of whom the greatest is Cervantes, she continually uses popular metaphorical expressions and expressive proverbs, some of which are traditional, while others she made up for herself.

Again, she is distinguished for her vivid metaphors, many of which have already been quoted. I am not, however, thinking here so much of the famous extended similitudes, amounting sometimes to allegories, as of the rapid, allusive figures which she throws off, almost unconsciously, as she goes: the Christian making progress 'at a hen's pace' or 'like hens with their feet tied';[27] his adversary the devil

[25] F. VII (III, 39).
[26] LL. 137 (November 19, 1576).
[27] L. XIII, XXXIX (I, 75–6, 284).

'clapping his hands to his head,' in despair of vanquishing him;[28] love finding an outlet and not being 'allowed to boil right over like a pot to which fuel has been applied indiscriminately';[29] and worldly aids to devotion being of no more use to lean upon than 'dry rosemary twigs'[30] which break at the slightest pressure. Between such inspired flashes and her classical similitudes come many striking images and illustrations, such as the picture of the donkey, working the water-wheel and drawing more water than the gardener,[31] or of the peasant-girl marrying the King.[32] Often, as a careful analysis of some of her longer illustrations will show, Teresa thinks in images, and the perusal of a list of all the figures she uses reveals a range nothing less than amazing in one of such comparatively restricted experience.

Such are the outstanding reasons for the high position which St. Teresa deservedly takes as a writer: many others could be found, and have been described by scholars, but these are paramount, and in a brief study they must suffice. It remains to be pointed out that, even more markedly than St. John of the Cross,[33] St. Teresa shows the diversity of her natural gifts by adapting her style to her subject. In the *Life* she is at her best in description, persuasive in argument and inclined to be leisurely and discursive throughout. In the *Way of Perfection*, her tone is decided, direct, even epigrammatic, with many exclamatory rhetorical questions and staccato passages. The *Foundations*, on the other hand, is all legato, frankly unhurried, with a tendency to long digressions—the diary, as it were, of a practised letter-writer. The *Interior Castle* is the weightiest of all; the work of an expositor; many of its figures are

[28] L. XXVI (I, 166).
[29] L. XXIX (I, 191).
[30] R. III (I, 316).
[31] L. XXII, (I, 142).
[32] *Conceptions*, III (II, 380).
[33] *Spirit of Flame*, p. 118.

carefully developed; sometimes it touches rare heights of eloquence; hardly ever does it sink to the conversational. The longest of the *Relations* resemble the finest passages in the *Life*. The *Conceptions* is essentially a series of meditations, some of which are intended to be read to others. The *Exclamations*, with their interrogatory and ejaculatory passages, their repetitions and their emphasis, could only be what they are—the breathings of a devout soul to God.

This chapter began with a quotation from the edition of Luis de León: it may appropriately end with another. Stressing Teresa's 'illumination and breadth of understanding in obscure and delicate spiritual matters' and her 'easy and pleasant way of writing of them,' he calls her 'the rarest of examples.'

> For in the sublimity of the subjects which she treats, and in the delicacy and charity with which she treats them, she surpasses many famous writers; while in the form of her writings, in the purity and ease of her style, in the gracefulness and skilful arrangement of the words and in an unaffected elegance which is delightful in the extreme, I doubt if there has been any writing of equal merit in our language.[34]

And, if we remember that these words first saw the light as early as the year 1588, we shall probably agree with him.

X

TERESA THE SAINT

ST. TERESA, as I have not hesitated to say elsewhere, was 'one of the most remarkable women who have ever lived,'[1] and to that small class she belongs by virtue of her character, her teaching and her gifts as a woman of affairs and as a writer. Of the many reasons for the vast extent of her appeal the most potent is probably her personality, and

---

[34] *Documents*, VII (C.W. III, 371–2).
[1] *Spirit of Flame*, p. 103.

this, in any account of her life, her foundations or her writings, stands out, quite irrespectively of the desire of the author that it should, high above everything else. For that very reason, we must guard against the risk of under-esteeming her doctrine. As a pure mystic, in the scientific sense of the word, she cannot, I think, be compared with St. John of the Cross, but her influence, if not so deep as his, is undoubtedly wider. He is 'the mystic's mystic';[2] she is 'a mystic—and more than a mystic.'[3] 'Her works, it is true, are well known in the cloister and have served as nourishment to many who are far advanced on the Way of Perfection, and who, without her aid, would still be begin-ners in the life of prayer. Yet they have also entered the homes of millions living in the world and have brought consolation, assurance, hope and strength to souls who, in the technical sense, know nothing of the life of contempla-tion.'[4] Everything she writes is based upon her own expe-rience, and so penetrating is her insight and so diaphanous her language that her readers can see themselves mirrored in her and interpret her experiences in terms of their own.

Her autobiographical, expository and hortatory pages blend to perfection. Where is the Christian who started his spiritual experiences at a lower point than she? Well may we prize those early chapters of the *Life*, describing the temptations of her girlhood, the gradualness with which she came to embrace the life of religion and the interior conflicts preceding the complete integration which she achieved at the age of about forty. Most of the mystics tell us something of the lowest stages of the ascent of Mount Carmel, but Teresa does more than that—she keeps us for a long time on the plain. They, even in their descriptions of the Way of Purgation, are apt to make us feel how much more heroic they are than we, and that feeling, in its turn, creates an inhibiting sense of frustration when we so much

[2] *Op. cit.*, pp. 16–19.
[3] C.W. I, 41.
[4] *Ibid.*

as glimpse the possibility of progressing farther. But she, leading us into the intimacy of those early days, when she 'took not the slightest trouble,' 'learned every kind of evil' and was 'seriously concerned' only about not being 'lost altogether,'[5] establishes a bond of sympathy with the reader and thus carries him with her all the way. And how carefully and fully charted a way! Sketched for us, in varying detail, in the little treatise on prayer embodied in the *Life*; elaborated in the *Conceptions of the Love of God* and the *Way of Perfection*; then re-drawn from beginning to end in the *Interior Castle*; and all the time illumined by what, in a pregnant phrase, though in another context, St. John of the Cross called 'lamps of fire'—the burning, as well as revealing, lights of the author's own experience.

If we add to all that the intense earnestness and sincerity of her language, which of itself enkindles, the simplicity of her often quite colloquial style and the attractiveness of her images, we shall begin to realize why to millions her position as a mystic is one of pre-eminence. No mystical writer before her time or since, says P. Silverio, 'has described such high matters in a way so apt, so natural and to such a large extent within the reach of all. The publication of her treatises inaugurated for the mystics an epoch of what may almost be termed popularity.'[6] And her appeal has not been confined to would-be contemplatives. All 'who love the pages of the Gospels, and whose aim in life is to attain the Gospel ideal of Christian perfection, have found in her works other pages in which, without any great effort of the intellect, they may learn much concerning the way.'[7] Of no true mystic can it be said that he is an unsocial Christian or unmindful of Our Lord's ethical teaching. But of St. Teresa such a thing would be said last, and least, of all. The ideal of the good life, the practice of the principles of the Sermon on the Mount, the develop-

[5] L. II (I, 14).
[6] C.W. I, xxxviii.
[7] *Ibid.*

ment of the cardinal virtues and the double duty of man, to God and to his neighbour—all these are constantly in her mind and inform her teaching.

But the chief power of that teaching is due, under God, to the magnetic personality by which it is inspired; and so, having paid tribute to the one, we may allow ourselves to contemplate the other—Teresa, as a person and as a saint. The picture gains immensely in clarity by its nearness in the gallery to the portrait of St. John of the Cross. The contrast between them strikes us from the moment when we first see them together: 'Teresa, the woman of fifty-two, her face lined by ill-health and austere discipline, but her humorous, sensitive mouth and her keen twinkling eyes testifying to her shrewdness and understanding of human nature. . . . Fray John, a diminutive boyish figure of five foot two inches, with the high forehead of the intellectual, the quiet, self-possessed mien of the man of character, the far-away expression of the visionary and the unfaltering and penetrating gaze of the mystic.'[8] That was in 1567. For five years the two see very little of each other, though he drinks deep from her experience and she from his spirituality. Then he comes to the Incarnation and becomes 'the father of her soul.'[9] They exchange spiritual confidences; probably they discuss her books while his own are yet unwritten. Thus, after less than two years of this happy fellowship, she leaves Ávila once more, while he remains until he is seized and thrown into prison. Thereafter they correspond, and occasionally their paths cross, but the period of their continuous contact is over. Yet unlike as in many ways they are, it is hard for those who know both, to read, or to read about, either of them, without thinking all the time of the other. In St. Teresa's works we continually find phrases, references, images which we come upon again in St. John of the Cross. In his detached and objective pages some anecdote, some reminiscence, recalls her

[8] *Spirit of Flame*, p. 21.
[9] LL. 261 (December 1578).

intensely personal narrative. Their characters are more curiously intertwined even than their writings. St. John, so gentle in his dealings with others, so enamoured of every kind of beauty, so graceful in his very turns of phrase, makes an initial impression which is positively feminine; yet one has not to penetrate far into his work and personality before coming to its flint-like core. St. Teresa, on the surface, is blunt, sometimes crude, uncompromising, stern, determined—masculine, in fact; yet, in her sensitiveness to the feelings of others, in her tender compassionateness, in her ready understanding, there was never a truer Mother.

The best conception of her personality is gained from a first-hand knowledge of her writings; and even from the brief account of her life and work given here the portrait will already have begun to disengage itself. Beginning with her girlhood, for example, we have traced her natural charm—that grace, as she put it, which the Lord had given her, wherever she was, to please people. And wherever she was, she did please people. The superficial attractiveness which she exercised as a girl developed into a gracious urbanity and a compelling, irresistible appeal. It moved great ladies to beg for her company; it worked upon soured and tantalized prelates; it captivated the General of the Order. 'I used,' she confesses, with characteristic frankness, 'to be very fond of being liked by others'[10] and that tendency, which she saw as a fault, she purified until it had turned into the corresponding virtue. That does not mean that she was ever in danger of becoming a 'frowning saint.' On the contrary, more than once in these pages we have heard her merry, ringing laugh and we may even have caught the quiet chuckle which she would give when something appealed to her sense of humour, and also, I fancy, when she contemplated external opposition, however fierce, against the background of a deep interior happiness. Gloomy nuns must indeed have been a trial to her. There is

[10] R. III (I, 316).

a most attractive passage near the end of the *Way of Perfection*, in which she warns her daughters against a censorious over-scrupulosity which takes the form of harsh judgments upon sisters who, 'in order to profit their neighbours, talk freely and without restraint.' If such persons, she exclaims, are 'of a lively disposition, you think them dissolute.... It is very wrong to think that everyone who does not follow in your own timorous footsteps has something the matter with her.'[11] And then St. Teresa's admonitions change from a negative to a positive key:

> Try, then, sisters, to be as pleasant as you can, without offending God, and to get on as well as you can with those you have to deal with, so that they may like talking to you and want to follow your way of life and conversation, and not be frightened and put off by virtue. This is very important for nuns: the holier they are, the more sociable they should be with their sisters. Although you may be very sorry if all your sisters' conversation is not just as you would like it to be, never keep aloof from them if you wish to help them and to have their love. We must try hard to be pleasant, and to humour the people we deal with and make them like us, especially our sisters.[12]

No less notable than her natural charm, and frequently, no doubt, in the eyes of her contemporaries, inseparable from it, are her utter simplicity, her deep sincerity and her hatred of every kind of pretentiousness. Even more than frowning saints, she must have detested self-conscious saints—the sort, as she puts it, who 'were saints in their own opinion, but, when I got to know them, they frightened me more than all the sinners I have ever met.'[13] She can muster an ironical smile at the self-importance of the world, where convention has so complicated the simple art of letter-writing that it can now be learned only from a course of lectures and will soon be demanding a university professorship.[14] 'Really the topsy-turviness of the world

[11] W.P. XLI (II, 181).
[12] *Ibid.*
[13] *Conceptions*, II (II, 375).
[14] L. XXXVII (I, 266).

is terrible.'[15] But when regard for 'nice points of honour' creeps into the religious life, she smiles no longer. 'It is enough . . . to make one weep.'[16] A sharp note comes into her voice as she chides nuns who feel slighted about 'things so trifling that they amaze me.' It is bad enough that learned doctors should have these artificial rules, according to which 'you must always be going up and never going down.'[17] But for poor nuns like themselves to observe such conventions is the work of the devil. Only he could have 'invented honours of his own for religious houses and . . . made laws by which we go up and down in rank, as people do in the world.'[18] 'God preserve us from religious houses where they worry about points of honour! Such places never do much honour to God.'[19]

That attitude is no affectation in a woman of such transparent sincerity. She has no wish to pose as virtuously imperturbable: sometimes 'the devil makes me so peevish and ill-tempered that I seem to want to snap everyone up.'[20] She has no intention of making a cheap reputation as a scholar: 'I am unable to use the proper terms.'[21] And she is equally honest and open about minor embarrassments —the kind of thing many a woman would try to hide. There was one of the earliest occasions, for instance, when she had to go and see a high-born lady. Where, in the autobiography of a saint, is there the like of this refreshing story?

It once happened to me, when I was not accustomed to addressing aristocrats, that I had to go on a matter of urgent business to see a lady who had to be addressed as 'Your Ladyship.' I was shown that word in writing; but I am stupid, and had never used such a term before; so when I arrived I got it wrong. So I decided to

[15] W.P. XXXVI (II, 155).
[16] W.P. XXXVI (II, 156).
[17] *Ibid.*
[18] *Ibid.*
[19] W.P. XXXVI (E) (II, 155).
[20] L. XXX (I, 199).
[21] L. XVIII (I, 106).

tell her about it and she laughed heartily and told me to be good enough to use the ordinary form of polite address, which I did.[22]

Then there is, of course, her virility, which stood out on the very first page of this narrative and will appear almost on the last. Of its source we cannot be sure. It may have developed during the years of childhood shared with her brother Rodrigo who was to die fighting in the Indies: if so, it remained latent until it was called forth by the over-powering determination to do at all costs the work to which she felt that God had called her. There is little sign of it in her girlhood, in her relations with her father during his last years or during the greater part of her life at the Incarnation. It seems not to appear until the moment when it is needed and thenceforward it appears everywhere—in her dealings with confessors, in her attitude to the Inquisi-tion, in her intransigence when faced by opposition, in her fearlessness before King, General, Bishops, aristocrats, and everyone else. She makes her decisions and is in no way appalled by their probable consequences:

> I was well aware that there was ample trouble in store for me, but, as the thing was now done, I cared very little about that.[23]

And the same manly note creeps into her letters, her prayers, her conversations, her exhortations to the nuns under her charge. One sentence from these might have been her epitaph:

> Strive like strong men until you die in the attempt, for you are here for nothing else than to strive.[24]

Charm, sincerity, virility—and, of course, sanctity. For Teresa's sanctity shone through all her actions, words and thoughts; through her journeyings and her foundations; through her visions and locutions; through her home-going,

[22] W.P. XXII (E) (II, 93–4).
[23] L. XXXVI (I, 253).
[24] W.P. XX (II, 86); cf. p. 78, above.

her influence and her fame. Yet I write of it, not first, but last, because to speak of it first might be to repel, whereas she herself always attracted. The light of saintliness is too strong for us unless we can approach it gradually, as Teresa's pilgrim approached the dazzling light of the innermost Mansion of the Castle. And that can be done only by getting to know the saint, first of all, as a person, so that, to a greater or a lesser extent, we may realize our kinship with the personality and lose the feeling that so lofty a soul belongs to another world than our own.

With St. Teresa, it is always to a greater extent. The fact that, but for Divine grace, she might have become so much like what we are makes us feel that, with the aid of Divine grace, we might become not unlike her. And, so far as one can tell from contemporary testimony, that was exactly the feeling which she inspired in those who knew her. She was just like themselves—only so much better! Her sanctity was never frightening; it always beckoned to itself.

Of course in those days nobody thought of her as we think today of a canonized saint, though they often described her as *santa*—a Spanish word which is not only a noun, but an adjective, meaning 'holy,' or, as we should say, 'good.' But that term was also applied with frequency to a very different type of person—'the pseudo-mystics of the day . . . with their ashen-pale countenances, their hands showing the marks of the stigmata, their fierce contortions and their periodical swoons.'[25] When Teresa protested, as she sometimes did, against its application to her, she may have been partly concerned to disown such shady connections. Nobody, however, even thought of likening her to them. The more ordinary were the people with whom she mingled, the more they were attracted by her plain, unaffected behaviour and speech. 'She was so natural and so courteous,' wrote a contemporary nun, with (I suppose) unconscious irony, 'that no one who looked at her would

[25] P. Silverio (C.W. III, xv).

think there was anything of the saint about her at all.'[26]
It was when you got to know her that you discovered the
difference. There was 'always something fundamental
about her,' reported the same nun, rather strikingly, 'which
forced even those who spoke ill of her to realize that she
was a saint without making any attempt to be.'[27] Something fundamental: affections deeply rooted, a life firmly
centred, a heart surely fixed. And nowhere was she better
than in little things. 'She was never idle,' says one, 'and
never at a loss for work to do.' 'She is very fond of engaging in the lowliest and humblest duties; and her companions assure me that, when it is her week to do the cooking,
they never lack for anything.'[28] And how could they? For,
said Teresa, *entre los pucheros anda el Señor*: 'the Lord
walks among the pots and pans,' just as much as in the
Garden of Eden, 'and He will help you in the tasks of the
inward life and of the outward life too.'[29]

But even those who failed to discern the Saint in Teresa
recognized the Mother. Her own nuns, first and foremost;
though distances were long and the primitiveness of transport made frequent visits to any one place impossible, the
consciousness of her spiritual presence was always with
them. 'They are so much like the nuns of St. Joseph's at
Ávila,' she wrote to her brother, Lorenzo, after she had
made six foundations, 'that they all seem one and the same
thing.'[30] And so it was everywhere. Scattered over the
country her nuns might be, but they were always members
of a single family, bound together, first of all, by the force
of her compelling and tender personality, and, after her
death, by the tradition which a career of only twenty years
had suffered to establish for all time.

[26] *Documents*, VI (III, 365–6).
[27] *Ibid.*
[28] *Documents* I (III, 326). St. Joseph's, Ávila, had no lay sisters on
its foundation, so the choir-nuns had to take their turns in the
kitchen.
[29] F. V (III, 22).
[30] LL. 19 (January 17, 1570).

'Our holy Mother,' she was called in those Carmels of Castile. 'Our holy Mother,' she is still called in Carmels all over the world today. And is she not also a Mother to many who will never be known as her daughters, but who in her blunt, frank counsels, reproofs and admonitions can hear a mother's voice? Never have there been more motherless children in need of her than today. If the fearless realism and the unflinching severity of St. John of the Cross speak to the world of tension and insecurity in tones which would have repelled it once but which it welcomes now, so too will the sincerity, the virility and the unpretentious, unaffected sanctity of St. Teresa. If we are to turn our backs upon the way of the world, which has failed us, and to seek a new world along the Way of Perfection, we shall do well to charter as our guides her writings, her ideals and her magnetic personality. And what the many must do now, the few have been doing for centuries; which is the reason 'why her name is not only graven upon the enduring marble of history but taken on the lips of generation after generation with reverence and love.'[31]

[31] P. Silverio (C.W. I, xxxvii).

INDEX

Numerous additional references to the Life, Foundations *and* Letters *of St. Teresa will be found in footnotes to this volume. Main references are printed throughout in heavy type.*

Active Life, 70, 71

Alba, Duchess of, 162

Alba de Tormes, 54, 102, 103, 109, 125, 148, 162, 163, 171

Alcalá de Henares, 87, 148, 155

Almodóvar, 123

Álvarez, P. Baltasar, 33, 37, 83, 86

Álvarez, P. Rodrigo, 62, 159

Ana de Jesús, 110, 168

Ana de San Bartolomé, 101, 151, 161, 162, 163, 164

Antonio de Jesús (Heredia), P., 84, 85, 86, 87, 89, 90, 151, 162

Arévalo, 84, 88

Aridity, 19, 56

Augustine, St., 24

Ávila, 9, 13, 15, 25, 26, 33, 35, 39, 41, 43, 48, 50, 62, 79, 82, 83, 84, 87, 89, 90, 91, 95, 97, 98, 99, 103, 109, 118, 120, 125, 132, 142, 147, 148, 153, 158, 159, 162, 175, 182, 188

Ávila, P. Julián de, 84, 85, 111, 115

Báñez, P. Domingo, 43, 48, 49, 58, 63, 87

Beas, 110–11

Beginners in prayer, 51, 52, 55, 134

Betrothal, Spiritual, 23, 106, 137, 141. *V. also* Mansions, Fifth.

Book-mark, St. Teresa's, 171

Burgo de Osma, 157, 158

Burgos, 125, 154, 160, 161, 162, 175

Calatrava, Order of, 93

Caravaca, 120

Carthusian Order, 87, 118

Castile, Castilian people and character, 9, 29, 36, 57, 111, 113, 120, 121, 140, 156, 177

Cepeda, Alonso (Sánchez) de, 10, 13, 15, 20–1

— (y Ahumada), Juana de, 39

— Lorenzo de, 118, 125, 154, 161, 168, 188

— María de, 13, 18

— Rodrigo de, 10, 11, 12, 186

— Teresa de. *V.* Teresa, St.

— Teresita de, 49, 153, 161, 169

Cerda, Luisa de la, 39, 40, 41, 48, 88, 89, 91, 109

Cervantes, Miguel de, 165, 177

Chess, game of, 65, 66, 70

Cicero, 10

Ciudad Real, 88

Conceptions of the Love of God, 22, 97, **105–8**, 178, 179, 181, 184

Consolations, Spiritual, 51, 135–6

Contemplation, 70, 71, 75, 133

Córdoba, 114, 116

Crashaw, Richard, 9, 11

Dalton, John, 165

David, King, 107

Diego de la Trinidad, P., 148

Dominican Order, 40, 43, 48, 58, 87, 124, 132

Doria, P. Nicolás, 153, 156, 158, 168

Duero, River, 156

Duruelo, 89, 90

Eboli, Princess of, 49, 93, 94

Ecija, 116

Ecstasy. *V.* rapture.

Escalona, 89

Escorial, El, 49, 63, 65, 76, 146

Exclamations of the Soul to God, 22, **95–7**, 170, 179

Fernández, P. Pedro, 124

Foundations, 22, 61, 79, 98, 100, 109, **124–30**, 145, 161, 169, 175, 176, 177

Francis Borgia, St., 26

Franciscan Order, 33, 47, 81, 92, 94, 118

General of Carmelite Order. *V.*

Rubeo
Gómez de Silva, Ruy, 93, 94
Gracian, P. Jerónimo, 48, 59, 100,
    102, 111–12', 121, 122, 123,
    124, 125, 130, 131, 132, 145,
    148, 149, 153, 155–6, 160,
    162, 168, 171
Graham, Gabriela Cunninghame,
    18
Granada, 110, 160
Granada, P. Luis de, 27, 177
Guadalajara, 93
Guadalquivir, River, 114
Guadarrama, Sierra de, 158

Hoornaert, P. Rodolphe, 47, 106

Incarnation, Convent of the
    (Ávila), 15, 17, 18, 19, 35, 37,
    41, 43, 44, 59, 70, 71, 103–5,
    109, 143–5
Inquisition, 39, 49, 54, 108, 131,
    186
Interior Castle, 22, 60, 62, 71,
    75, 76, 77, 97, 130–42', 145,
    165, 166, 178, 181
— compared with Life, 46, 170

Jesus, Society of, 24, 25, 26, 30,
    32, 34, 39, 50, 60, 74, 83, 98,
    124
John of the Cross, St., 27, 51,
    59, 87, 90, 96, 105, 110, 139,
    141, 143, 145, 147, 162, 166,
    169, 175, 178, 180, 181, 182,
    189
— compared with St. Teresa,
    182
José de Cristo, P., 90
Joseph, Covent of St. (Ávila),
    36, 41–5, 48, 50, 62, 64, 66,
    68, 69, 70, 79, 81, 83, 87, 89,
    91, 103, 110, 120, 142, 143,
    159, 162, 173, 188
Juan de los Ángeles, P., 27
Juan de Jesús (Roca), P., 148

Laredo, Bernardino de, 47
Latin, St. Teresa and, 177
Leon, P. Luis de, 58, 64, 95, 108,
    165, 179
Letters (of St. Teresa), 59,
    168–9
Lewis, David, 165

Life, 22, 45, 46–61, 67, 75, 108,
    130, 131, 136, 141, 165, 178,
    180, 181, 185
Locutions, 29, 30, 36, 50, 53, 118,
    161
Lord's Prayer, 75–7, 97
Lutherans, 78

Madrid, 87, 90, 91, 94
Malagón, 88, 93, 120, 124, 149,
    150, 152
Malone, William, 165
Mancha, La, 150
Mansions, First, 134; Second,
    134; Third, 134; Fourth,
    135–6, 137, 139; Fifth, 23,
    137–8; Sixth, 139–40; Seventh,
    86, 137, 140–1, 159, 187
María de San Jerónimo, 147
María de San José, 100, 108, 113,
    114, 144, 148, 149, 159, 177
María del Sacramento, 98–9
Marriage, Spiritual, 96, 106, 137,
    140–1
Mascareñas, Leonor de, 87
Mathew, Tobias, 165
Medina del Campo, 83, 84, 86,
    87, 88, 89, 98, 99, 103, 109,
    147, 148, 151, 153, 160, 162
Meditation, 19, 56, 71, 134, 135
Mendoza, Álvaro de (Bishop of
    Ávila and later of Palencia),
    41, 82, 142, 152, 153
Mendoza, María de, 90
Mental prayer, 20, 21, 22, 34, 44,
    73–4. V. also Contemplation,
    Meditation.
Moraleja, La, 123
Morena, Sierra, 112

Navarre, 156

Ocampo, María de, 35
Ormaneto, P. Niccolo, 121, 123,
    143
Osuna, P. Francisco de, 18, 19,
    20, 27, 56

Padilla, Casilda de, 128–9
Palencia, 60, 143, 152, 154, 155,
    156, 157, 158, 160, 162
Pastrana, 93, 94, 95, 109, 111,
    148
Peñaranda, 163

Peter of Alcántara, St., **33–5**, 40, 41, 44
Philip II, King, 91, 120, 124, 143, 145, 146, 148
Piacenza, 120, 121
Poems (of St. Teresa), 170–5
Purgation, 55, 56, 134, 180

Quiet, Prayer of, 18, 19, 23, 56, 67, 75, 76, 106, 135, 136

Rapture, Ecstasy and, 57, 139
Recollection, Prayer of, 66, 75, 76, 136
Relations, Spiritual, 23, **58–61**, 96, 109, 112, 123, 136, 142, 143, 157, 158, 159, 178, 179, 183
Ribera, P. Francisco de, 11, 17, 132, 147
Ripalda, P. Jerónimo, 124, 154, 156, 161
Roda, La, 150
Rome, 123, 145, 148
Rubeo, P. Juan Bautista, 81, 82, 83, 103, 117, 121, 122, 124, 125, 183

Salamanca, 87, 97–9, 103, 109, 124, 148, 149
Salazar, P. Gaspar de, 39
Scripture, St. Teresa and, 107
Sega, P. Filippo, 103, 123, 143, 148
Segovia, 95, 109, 132, 154, 158, 159
Seville, 60, 110, 112, **116–19**, 120, 144, 147, 149, 151, 153
Silkworm, similitude of the, 137–8
Silverio de Santa Teresa, P., 46, 97, 133, 165, 168, 181, 187, 189
Song of Solomon, 106, 107, 108
Soria, 156–8, 159
Stanbrook, Benedictines of, 18, 65, 165

Teresa, St. Common-sense, 52, 70–1, 107; humour, 38, 52, 183; intimacy with God, 53; memory, 167; metaphors, use of, 58, 64–5, 71–2, 75–6, 97, 141–2, 170, **177**; realism, 52; sanctity, 186–9; sincerity, 185; style, 58, 64, 77, 125–8, 166, 168, **176–8**; virility, 52, 72, 78–9, 177, 186; for references to the main incidents of St. Teresa's life, *v.* pp. 5–6.
Toledo, 39, 41, 48, 60, 88, 89, 90, 91, 92, 93, 95, 97, 105, 120, 124, 132, 142, 147, 150, 153
Tostado, P. Jerónimo, 121, 123, 144, 145, 146
Transverberation of the Heart (of St. Teresa), 32
Travels, description of St. Teresa's, **100–2**, 113, 158, 161–2

Ubeda, 112
Ulloa, Guiomar de, 33, 35
Union, 19, 57, 58, 74–5. *V. also* Mansions, Seventh; Marriage, Spiritual.
Union, Prayer of. See Betrothal, Spiritual.

Valladolid, 63, 65, 89, 90, 91, 148, 153, 154, 156, 160, 162, 175
Velázquez, Alonso (Bishop of Osma), 60, 131, 157, 159, 169
Villanueva de la Jara, 150–3
Virgil, 10
Visions, St. Teresa's, 23, 30, 31, 32, 54, 141
Vocal prayer, 75, 76

Water, Similitude of, 24, 51, 54, 59, 72, 135–6, 141–2
Waters, Four, 50, **54–8**, 97, 134, 139; First Water, 55, 56, 134; Second —, 55, 56; Third —, 55, 56, 73, 137, 141; Fourth —, 55, 56, 57, 73, 141
Way of Perfection, 22, **61–79**, 97, 107, 126, 127, 131, 135, 136, 167, 178, 181, 184, 185, 186
Woodhead, Abraham, 165

Yanguas, P. Diego de, 108, 132
Yepes, P. Diego de, 130, 132
Zimmerman, P. Benedict, 166